SOMETHING UNSETTLING IS TAKING PLACE AT MIDWAY POSTAL STATION...

*W*ith high expectations from her father weighing heavily on her back, the privileged Cadina Wilson enters the postal system as a new employee only to be confronted with immediate drama from her coworkers and management, such as...

...the self-destructing alcoholic Freeman Souls, who must decide to either stay in a troublesome relationship with his fiancée, or start a new and exciting venture with the gorgeous, yet mysterious, Velour Patterns...

...the arrogant Lexington VanGuard and his power-tripping tendencies as he relishes the opportunity to become a career supervisor...

...newly appointed Assistant Manager Denise Tucker, who finds herself being brutally challenged by her manipulative boss, the charming Michael Davenport...

...the devoted father, James Richards, who desperately seeks custody of his daughter Janae while falling in love all at once...

...And it won't be long before Cadina's path takes an unexpected turn when she is plunged inside everyone's unstable world. But when a bitter employee makes a startling discovery, all hell really begins to break loose...

"The language and the characters of *Postal* are not only believable, but they have roots. Therefore, they earn a spot in the readers' hearts. Here, the reader will discover that the *seemingly simple* average American working class is both complex and significant.

–Gladys E. Perez-Bashier, Publisher and Co-Founder of Clique Calm Books, Author of Creepin' Through the Hinge

"The author's depiction of the melting pot of postal employees was very accurate. He gave another perception of the postal service; a more humanistic side versus us as just 'keepers of the mail'. I thoroughly enjoyed reading it."

–Barbara Parker Reid, U.S.P.S. Window Clerk

"An extremely entertaining story threaded with life lessons that any person, postal-employed or not, can relate to. I was very impressed...GREAT JOB!"

–Yvonne Mullins, U.S.P.S. Customer Service Manager

POSTAL REBOOT

Peter McNeil

This is a work of fiction. Names, characters, businesses, places, events, locales, and incidents are either the products of the author's imagination or used in a fictitious manner. Any resemblance to actual persons, living or dead, or actual events is purely coincidental.

Category: Fiction
Edition: Third
Specifications: Softcover
ISBN Number: 978-0-9856990-3-1
Date of Publication: 6/1/2022
Cover Design by Charlton "CP the Artist" Palmer

Copyright © 2022 by Peter McNeil

All Rights Reserved. No part of this publication may be reproduced, stored in a retrieval system, or transmitted, in any form or in any means - by electronic, mechanical, photocopying, recording, or otherwise - without prior written permission. For information regarding permission, contact Peter McNeil at postaltheseries@gmail.com and peter2539@att.net.

A BRIGHTER PATH PRODUCTIONS

Acknowledgments

To our Creator, I give thanks for the gift instilled in me to share with the world. An angel was sent to me in the form of my wife, Pamela Smith-McNeil. I thank God every day for her immeasurable love, friendship, never-ending support, words of wisdom, sincere criticism, being the mother and educator of our children, and her culinary skills! (Love ya, honey!) To my children, Justin, Jordan, and Milahn, who have always taken interest in what I was accomplishing and for being my motivation factors, as well; I love y'all. To my mother, Lucille McNeil, thank you for adopting me and my brother Kevin, love you, and may you both rest in peace. My sister Mary-Lee Wright, thank you so much for being that positive nurturer. To the rest of my family, in-laws, and friends, thanks for all the support and encouragement (So many of you, I had to break it down like that!)

Now, for the Dream Team that made it all possible....

Editor Denise Spiller, for recommending that I switch my project from a screenplay to the page-turner it has become. I'm forever grateful for that suggestion. My editors for the book, Gladys "Poppi" Perez-Bashier, Sandra Kendall, and my wife Pam, thank you for providing my novel the necessary polish it needed. Charlton "CP the Artist" Palmer, thank you for blessing me with eye-popping, attention-grabbing book covers and business logos, I'm forever grateful. To my personal book critics, Yvonne Mullins, Barbara Parker-Reid, and Tashia "Flossie Mae" Smith, for giving me the constructive feedback I needed to ensure the subject matters that I've tackled were properly represented.

Last, but not least, Morgan Postal Processing Station in Midtown Manhattan, Cooper Postal Station in Lower Eastside Manhattan, and Hell Gate Post Office in East Harlem; you were the catalyst for my decision to become a writer. My postal experience provided me the platform to not only give the reader insight into the postal environment but also life experiences and I sincerely thank you.

This was definitely a labor of love and commitment. Hope you will enjoy it.

Pete McNeil

POSTAL REBOOT

--------- a Novel by ---------

PETER MCNEIL

To the dedicated, hard-working, and colorful
postal employees all over the world...
I salute you.

JANUARY 2016

❄ ❄ WINTER'S HARVEST ❄ ❄

VELOUR PATTERNS

*D*avenport clears his throat and in a booming voice says, "Good morning, ladies and gentlemen of Midway. I don't want to take up too much of your time…we have a lot of mail on the way to our station, so I'll make this as brief as I can. But first, I want to commend you all for last week's performance. The mail volume was exceptionally high and all of you really came through like the professionals that you are. I even tip my hat off to the ones who are not on the overtime list. You really made a difference, especially when our station's roster is short-staffed. Thank you for a job well done."

Letter Carrier Velour Patterns listens while she analyzes Michael Davenport, Midway Station's influential manager. With his shiny dark bald head, charismatic eyes, and pearly-white teeth, Davenport's overwhelming charm cannot be denied. Yet, every employee in the building can see right through those super-tight smiles and exaggerated laughs. He loves the power he has and does not short himself when it comes to using it. The only thing that is as big as his oversized ego is his massive, towering physique, which today, is underneath a dark blue pinstripe suit. This adds to his intimidating stature. Not one person has questioned him regarding his handling of the station's very few inadequate carriers. He has even shown supervisors a thing or two about how to take control of their designated sections, while at the same time, demeaning them right in front of employees, during the process. About the only one who has come close to challenging his aggressive nature is his assistant, Denise Tucker, who vehemently disapproves of his bullying tactics most times. Afterward, she usually backs down and walks away, saving her critical opinions until they are behind closed doors. No one else, however, must be reminded of who oversees Midway Postal Station.

Velour smirks at the manager.

He wishes he was the only charmer in the building.

She glances around the postal congregation with eyes probing in search of her primary target.

Hmmm, he must be still out on the road.

Instead, her eyes land upon the primary target's nosy little sister, Divine Souls, who is busy thumbing on her cell phone. Probably texting her brother about the morning meeting. Divine loves her brother dearly; it is well known throughout the workplace.

I would love for your brother to fuck the shit out of me, but that's none of your business, little girl.

As if she was reading Velour's mind, Divine's head pops up and their eyes connect.

Velour seductively crosses her legs and smiles at the little brat.

Divine shoots her a dark look before resuming to her phone.

Velour snickers to herself and turns her attention back to the manager.

"Now, some of you may have already read about this in the news, but for those who haven't, a letter carrier across town was caught trashing mail inside dumpsters on his temporary assignment over a five-day span last month. A customer recorded the carrier in the act and notified the Postmaster." Davenport pauses to allow his staff to digest that last statement. "This has become a disturbing trend in the past two years. Now, the Inspecting General is taking profound measures to make sure these senseless acts don't become an epidemic. That employee is now charged with Obstruction of Correspondence, which is a federal offense, and will possibly face two years in prison. He may pay fines, as well. The Postal Service will no longer tolerate any displays of reckless behavior that damages the code of ethics which all of you dedicated individuals work extremely hard to preserve."

Divine raises her hand.

"Yes, Divine..."

"Was the carrier a new employee?"

"Yes, he was, and his actions have prompted the Postal Academy to be more critical in their selection of candidates. They're also providing additional training and reinforcing our code of conduct policy."

Velour raises her hand.

Davenport points to Velour. "Yes..."

"Not to switch subjects, but what is being done about the carrier shortage around here? Especially since the other two new hires quit last month. It's getting ridiculous."

"Well, that was to be my concluding discussion. As it so happens, we have a new sub arriving first thing in the morning."

"Just one?"

"You have to crawl before you walk, my dear."

"But that's our problem; we've been crawling for like a whole year now, it's time to take the baton and start running!"

The audience laughs.

Most of the male employees overdo it just because it's her.

Velour smiles, knowing she is the only person in the station that can steal the spotlight from the manager with no effort at all. From the corner of her eye, she catches Divine rolling her eyes.

"We will, I promise you." smiles Davenport. "And she will be assigned to your section, so I expect all of you to be of great support to her. She'll need it. Now, are there any more questions? No? Alright. Everyone, have a safe and pleasant delivery. And again, thank you for last week's effort. It's greatly appreciated."

Carriers snatch up their stools and head back to their assigned sections, privately bickering to themselves or among other carriers about the meeting's topics.

Velour picks up her stool and strolls toward her workstation. A couple of male coworkers vie for her attention. She calmly waves at them as if she was a reigning beauty pageant winner. They eagerly wave back. She gets a kick out of their thirsty expressions.

Velour takes a deep breath as she surveys the mountain of mail that she and her route partner, Dante, have to case up today on their business route. Twenty buckets of magazines, large envelopes, and packages, as well as fifteen letter trays. And more mail is on the way. Most of the bulk mail was left behind yesterday due to her feeling under the weather and leaving to go home early. Dante, on the other hand, was very outspoken about her decision.

Fuck him, he'll be alright.

Velour grabs a handful of letters and begins casing. While sorting, one piece of mail catches her eye—an envelope addressed to one of her customers, Ms. Havana Blunt, a wealthy widow who enjoys an international vacation every chance she gets.

She presses her fingers all around the envelope.

Feels like a credit card.

Hmmm.

She discreetly glances around her area.

Everyone is tending to their own business.

She purposely drops the envelope on the floor. Next to her feet is her personal shoulder bag, which is already opened. She quickly scans her surroundings before she bends down, scoops up the envelope, and then drops it into the opened bag. She then pushes the bag to the side with her foot.

Again, she looks around to see if anyone is watching.

No one is paying her any attention.

But someone catches *her* eye.

He just arrived on the work floor, taking off his postal jacket, and headed toward her with a small brown bag—probably the oatmeal he said he was going to buy her.

He smiles.

She blushes.

I wonder if he smiles at his fiancée the same way he smiles at me.

FREEMAN SOULS

*D*IVINE'S TEXT MESSAGE – *DID YOU FORGET ABOUT THE MANDATORY MEETING? WHERE YOU AT?*

He pockets his phone and quickly screws the cap back on his silver liquor flask. He downs an Aquafina water bottle, followed by four peppermints. He cups his mouth and breathes. *Satisfied.* Finally, he cranks the postal truck and motors down Lafayette Street.

Letter Carrier Freeman Souls could get used to driving the postal truck for the rest of his career. He loves the position so much that he is seriously considering putting his bid in for the truck assignment he is temporarily assigned to. But in his gut, he knows he has a better chance of winning the state's lottery than getting selected over the other bidders who have way more seniority than he. In fact, those same bidding letter carriers, who he often catches peeking in and around his truck, always find the time to go out of their way to inquire about the truck's setup.

"Freeman! Uh, how long does it take for you to do the early drops? Hey, Freeman! How do you deliver to buildings that usually receive large sums of mail, but no service elevators and only one small passenger elevator? Yo, Free! Did the customers tip you well this past Christmas?"

These are all the questions he has been hearing for the past month and he will continue to hear those kinds of inquiries until one of those eager carriers is selected for the truck permanently.

His sweet, but temporary, assignment is ending real soon and when that fateful day arrives, he is going to be placed right back in his assigned section as a reluctant foot soldier, bouncing from route to route, sometimes cleaning up other letter carriers' messes, and often staying out to deliver mail until the sun settles and the moon pops up. And if that does not irk his nerves, there is always the potential threat of getting transferred to another station. That is what they do to unassigned letter carriers who have been appointed regular status after serving two years as a Part-Time Flexible Substitute, a PTFS, or a sub for short.

The very thought makes him cringe.

It so happens that he does not envision himself going anywhere, anytime soon. The Brooklyn-born-but-now-Bronx-residing letter carrier has feverishly grown fond of the Lower East Side Village area in downtown Manhattan where the station is located. The area is rich with so much ethnic culture and media background, he wonders why he never frequented this section of Manhattan before. From the NYU dormitories which houses students from all walks of life to the swarms of celebrities, who constantly roam the village to tie deals and dine in the finest restaurants –the place is a twenty-four-hour global networking magnet. And on any given day or night, you might find a film crew shooting a scene for a big-budget movie. No, he would not trade this scenery for the world.

And it does not end there. The solid relationships he has built over the past two years at Midway Postal Station, he can't picture duplicating anywhere else. Even the station's manager, Davenport, is making it his business to persuade him into taking the supervisor's exam and joining his elite managerial staff. Freeman, as usual, laughs it off and keeps it moving.

His assistant manager, Tucker, adores him as well. However, lately, she has been constantly reminding him about his recent work performance and attendance, which in her eyes, have both been substandard at best.

Although he is fond of his assistant manager's motherly approach, he does not need another mother figure in his life. The woman who birthed him thirty-three years ago succumbed to a hit and run late last year and the pain of that tragedy is as fresh as if he'd just received the phone call of her death only minutes ago. What he needs is to be on this temporary driving assignment so he can grieve by his lonesome. He also revamped his Hennessy indulgence, which was conquered a few years back when he started going back to his family church. Unfortunately, right after his mother's funeral, the Henny started creeping back into his life, and church became a distant afterthought. No, he does not need another mother figure lecturing him. He would love to have his old one back.

His cell phone vibrates as he approaches a red light.

He knows exactly who it is, but he reads the name on the screen, anyway.

His fiancée, Lovelle...just as he thought.

The light turns green, he lifts his foot from the brake and allows the voicemail to receive the message. At the next light, he decides to listen:

"Hey, baby, it's me. Hope you're having a beautiful morning. Give me a call when you have a moment, I want to go over with you the guestlist for our wedding and I also want to-"

He erases the voicemail and places the phone back on his hip.

He parks the truck on the corner of East Seventeenth Street and hops out to empty the final collection box. The ice-cold January temperature does not hamper his responsibility as he opens the blue box with his arrow key and rakes the overflowing mail into his large mailbag.

A gloved finger taps him on his shoulder.

He spins around defensively, causing the startled woman to take a cautious step back.

"I'm sorry, I didn't mean to appear aggressive," he says.

"Nooo, that's quite alright," smiles the briefcase-toting lady. "I'm the one who should be apologizing for sneaking up on you the way I did."

"Oh, no apology necessary."

He awkwardly gawks over the attractive sista, stylishly dressed in winter corporate wear. He softens his stance.

Corporate Lady sticks out her gloved hand, which holds a couple of letters. "Could you make sure my bills make it to their destination on time? I wouldn't want to hunt you down because they charged me a late fee."

Her smiling eyes are as direct as her come on.

He fights hard not to give in.

"Can't have that, right?" he replies. "But you have yourself a beautiful day, Mrs.—" He quickly reads the letters. "Thompson."

"That's *Miss* Thompson," she states while holding onto his hand. "And you do the same."

Corporate Lady winks, turns around, and then struts her assets around the corner.

He shakes off the vibe and regains his composure.

Hell, I'ma put my bid in for this truck assignment anyway–later for them.

He nods in response to his thoughts, slams the mailbox shut, leaps inside his truck, dumps the mail inside the tub with all the other mail, and motors back to Midway Station.

Freeman backs the truck up against the loading dock and unloads two rolling tubs of collection mail onto the platform. One of the mail-handlers greets Freeman, takes the tubs, and pushes them right up against the other tubs of mail near the brick wall. He grabs a small brown bag, locks the truck, and walks inside the station.

Entering Sterling's office, he hands over his collection box scanner to the truck supervisor/computer specialist who quickly snatches it and returns to punching away at his computer keyboard. The white-frazzle-haired supervisor appears bothered by something.

"Everything alright?"

Sterling downloads Freeman's scanner information into the computer. "You would think after sixteen years, I wouldn't still be correcting others' mistakes."

Freeman cops a squat in a nearby folding chair. "Uh-oh. Who let you down this time?"

"Our boss caused quite a stir with the senior carriers' vacation bids. Now, I have the displeasure of going back into the system to undo what he's done. Word of warning, Freeman; you can forget about the Fourth of July week."

"I'm not worried about that. I'll take whatever I can get."

Sterling stops typing. He raises his droopy eyes to look at him. "That's a first. When a sub turns to regular status, they usually start demanding the most sought-after vacation slots. Should I be concerned about your mental health?"

Freeman smiles. He then peeks at the computer screen. "How do I look?"

Sterling reads the data from Freeman's scanner and points to the screen. "You forgot to scan this box, see, right here…"

Frowning, Freeman moves in closer to the computer. "Where?"

"Your last box, East Seventeenth Street. Are you sure your mind wasn't pre-occupied?"

"I don't think so," Freeman lies, thinking about the sexy corporate lady. "Damn, I hate going back out there during rush hour."

Sterling chuckles. "Don't worry about it now. You have an emergency meeting to attend upstairs."

Freeman reaches for his scanner. "I bet I know what it's pertaining to."

Sterling leans over his stack of manuals to grab the Daily Newspaper. The front-page headline reads: MAILMAN DUMPING MAIL!

"It's starting to be a trend all over the country," Sterling says, flipping through the paper to find the article.

"I bet. Later." Freeman rises from the chair and leaves the office.

"Don't forget to scan the box after the meeting!" is all he hears from the truck supervisor.

"I WON'T!"

Freeman races up the staircase, taking two steps at a time. He arrives on the "carrier work floor" and glances around at the scene in front of him. Carriers returning to their workstations, mailhandlers dispersing mail, and managers talking to supervisors.

Damn. Missed another meeting.

Freeman sighs while peeling out of his postal jacket. He makes his way toward Section C when he sees Velour, who is bending down in front of her workstation. His mood brightens immediately.

When she stands, she glances his way.

Their eyes intertwine.

He feels as though he is walking in slow motion. This dropdead gorgeous woman, with a blond flip hairdo and tight, mouthwatering light-skinned voluptuous figure, sticks her tongue out at him like a bratty schoolgirl. He mimics her actions.

He walks up to her and reaches the small brown bag towards her.

"You may have to heat the oatmeal up," he says. "I bought it before I started my collection run, so-"

"It's alright," she says, placing the bag to the side. "I plan on eating it on break, anyway. But thank you so much."

"I'ma holla at my sis, I'll be right back."

"Okay."

His body fails to obey his plan. Her Dentyne smile has him captivated.

"Uh, see you in a minute."

Velour laughs. "You know where I'll be."

He breaks out of his trance and walks over to Divine's workstation, tosses his jacket over a bucket of Sports Illustrated magazines, and plops down on her stool. He watches as Divine cases the letters at a steady pace and then surveys her mail for the day. Fifteen full letter trays and fifteen buckets of oversized envelopes, magazines, and third-class bulk mail combined. He remembers a year ago when he was stuck on this dreadfully long route. *Hated it!* He does not miss it for the world. But now, his little sister suffers the same agony, day in and day out. She is in for an exceptionally long day.

Divine side-eyes him as she sorts the mail. "And yet, he somehow manages to miss another mandatory meeting."

"I got tied up in traffic during my collection run, what you want me to do-"

"Same excuse, all the time."

"What did I miss?"

She reaches to the side to snatch the Daily Newspaper. She points to the headline, MAILMAN DUMPING MAIL!

"Yeah, I read about that earlier."

"This makes us look more like fools by the day." She resumes casing the mail. "I don't understand why it's so difficult to just bring the mail back to the station and quit if you can't handle the job. That's all they gotta do! Makes no sense at all."

Even though she can be a pain in the ass, Freeman has always admired his little sister. A lot of their mother's values are instilled in her, which makes her a wise old owl at the tender age of twenty-five. She also has their mother's mouth, which, at times, is a force to be reckoned with. But other than that, he applauds her rock-hard fortitude, especially when it comes to her dedication to church. Although this job may require her to work ten to twelve-hour days, six days a week, she still manages to make it to Wednesday night bible study and Saturday night choir rehearsal. On Sunday, her only day off during her probation period, she spends the entire day with her church family in the Lord's house. That is dedication to a fault. She's stuck on a dismal route that nobody in their right mind would bid on, yet she makes the necessary adjustments to do it all.

"I see you settling into your regular status rather well," Divine says. "What's it been, three weeks already?"

"Something like that. And I'm an *unassigned* regular. So, I still can't get too comfortable around here."

"Seems like you're already cozy in your position if you ask me." Her words take on a more scornful tone now. "You come and go as you please. I don't get to talk to you like I want to, especially since you don't come to church anymore–"

"Is there a point to be made out of all of this?"

She pauses sorting and glares at him. "Yes, it is. I want to know why you stopped coming out to check on me during my heavy delivery days?"

"Huh?"

"You heard me...you know this route requires auxiliary assistance almost every single day, and today will be no different–"

"What are you talking about? Chapman sends people out left and right to make sure you're not out there all night-"

"But that wouldn't have stopped you before." Divine resumes sorting the mail. "You're so worried about Miss Thang over there that you forgot all about your sister."

Finally, it is out in the open.

He cannot deny the fact that Miss Thang, a.k.a. Velour Patterns, has taken precedence over Divine in the past couple of months. A once reserved carrier who didn't have two words to say to him when he first arrived at the station, all of a sudden, has opened up and become quite attentive to him, especially after his mother's passing. The relationship has matured to the point where the entire station is declaring the two an item. Freeman does not mind the gossip. He welcomes a refreshing presence in his turbulent life.

And justifying his every move with his kid sister is becoming a rather dull task.

"Oh, now I see where this is leading."

"That is a two-man route over there, Freeman. She and Dante are supposed to help each other, but they choose not to. And just because she says "hi" to you and wiggle her big behind all in your face, you're supposed to feel obligated to race over and help her? She doesn't even need it!"

"Here we go…"

"Well, it's true."

"What is it you got against Velour, anyway?"

She rolls her eyes but says nothing as she stuffs letters into the route-case.

"Oh, cat got your tongue now, huh? Has it ever occurred to you that maybe Velour is cool people? And you'd know that if you ever decide to get off your high horse and have a conversation with her."

"Oh, okay. But keep in mind you're engaged to one of my closest friends, alright? And why are you always up in Velour's face, anyway? What's that all about?"

"Mind your business, alright?"

"Yeah, whatever."

"FREEMAN!" Davenport yells from the supervisor's podium. "A MOMENT OF YOUR TIME, PLEASE."

"See!" Divine quips. "You should've made it to the meeting this morning-"

"Shut up."

Freeman leaves his sister's workstation but then stops short.

He discreetly turns around and cups his mouth to check his breath.

Good to go.

He walks over to the podium where Davenport is waiting.

The tall manager smiles and shakes Freeman's hand. "My *main* man…"

"Sorry I couldn't make it back to the meeting. Traffic was a beast out there."

Davenport waves him off. "Don't worry about that, son. I need a favor from you."

"Sure. What's up?"

"We're getting a new employee tomorrow and I want you to train her on the truck assignment. She needs to learn everything; collections, early drop-offs, relays–and fast. Can I count on you?"

"I gotcha covered."

Davenport beams with pride. "My man. Now, what's this I hear about you becoming a supervisor?"

Confusion drapes Freeman's expression. "And who told you that?"

"I did."

Freeman turns around and frowns at Letter Carrier Lexington VanGuard. The dark-skinned, bald head, ass-kissing protégé of Davenport struts right up to their conversation, decked out in a dark blue pinstripe suit, mimicking the station manager's appearance to the tee.

Lexington grins at Freeman. "I told Mr. Davenport you were thinking about applying for the next supervisor exam. Need I say it brought a smile to his face."

"Sure did," Davenport adds.

"The thought did cross my mind, but that was the extent of it," Freeman explains to Davenport while keeping his eyes on Lexington. "I have no intentions of becoming a supervisor. I'm good where I'm at."

Lexington's eyes darken for a split second before he re-establishes his shit-eating grin. "Well, I guess I misunderstood you, Freeman."

"It wouldn't be the first time."

"That's too bad," Davenport says, in good spirits. "But if you ever reconsider, my door is always open for mentorship. Lexington can attest to that, right, son?"

"Don't overlook this opportunity, Freeman."

Freeman's glare is his only response to the bald nitwit.

Davenport checks his watch. "And on that note, I have a meeting to attend uptown. Freeman, thanks again for your commitment for tomorrow."

Davenport slips on his gray wool coat, dons his black Indiana Jones Stetson hat, grabs his briefcase, and commandingly marches down the work floor.

Lexington beams with pride as he stares at the manager disappearing through the stairwell. That beam-with-pride smile evaporates when he faces Freeman. "Do you even have a clue on what you're passing up, bruh?"

Freeman often wonders if giving Lexington a supervisor title would prove to be a good thing in the long run. Sure, he might pass the exam easily and he could impress the board members, but it disturbs him that a person like Lex would receive that kind of authority when he is already cursed with raw arrogance which flows through his veins like dope. He has a nasty tendency of cutting people off mid-sentence; and when he speaks to someone, it is always with an annoying, superior attitude. He tries to give Lexington the benefit of the doubt, but it is difficult to reach deep inside of a person's soul, like Lexington, and bring out the good because he, in essence, doesn't really have anything positive to say about anybody, other than himself–and Davenport, of course. And Freeman knows better than to think that Lexington sincerely appreciates their friendship, but the Lord does say to "Love Thy Neighbor."

The Lord is asking for a lot.

Freeman keeps an even tone. "I want to know when I appointed you to become my spokesperson, Lex-?"

"Never mind that," Lexington snaps, cutting Freeman off. "We're talking straight leveling up, dude–fuck this letter carrier shit, ain't nothing prestigious about that position! Unless you're afraid of what people may think of you crossing over to management…is that the case?"

"That's none of your concern."

Lexington shakes his head. "Here I am thinking we're on the same trajectory with our careers because we started out together, but now I see you're no different than the rest of these cats around here–"

"And *maybe* we're not cut from the same cloth, Lex. You're already power-tripping and you're not even a supervisor yet!"

He could tell that struck a chord with Lexington. The idiot's jaws clenched.

"In three months, they're having another supervisor's exam." He leans in closer to Freeman's face. "Do yourself a favor and get with the program because this is not you…*capisce*? Now, if you'll excuse me, I have to change."

A displeased Lexington turns around and heads toward the stairwell.

Hurrying past Lexington and speed-walking straight to Freeman is Velour's route partner, Dante Maxwell, carrying a bucket of mail. He's not displaying a positive disposition at all.

"You need to talk to your girl, Free," Dante seethes, passing Freeman without breaking a stride.

Here we go.

Freeman follows the disgruntled coworker to his workstation.

Dante also passes by Velour without saying a word. He drops the bucket of mail to the ground and then grabs a bundle of Time magazines to sort. While angrily flinging each magazine into its designated slot, Dante turns to Freeman. "She's gonna need your assistance, you already know this. *Look* at all this shit. I'm not lifting one finger to help her out-"

"We can handle it, Freeman." She shoots Dante a dirty look. "I don't know why he's tripping; he knew I was under the weather yesterday-"

"Because we should've dealt with all of this bulk mail yesterday instead of leaving it for today, that's why!" Dante snatches up another bundle of magazines to sort. "Now Daphne is gonna wind up taking our boys to football practice *again* because I'll be two hours late getting home. This is bullshit and you know it!"

"Well, that sounds like a personal problem to me."

Dante whips his head around to face Freeman. He motions with his hands as if to say, *you see the shit I have to put up with, right?*

The intercom blares out Freeman's name. "FREEMAN SOULS, IF YOU'RE STILL IN THE BUILDING, REPORT TO MY OFFICE WITH YOUR SCANNER. THANK YOU."

Freeman says, "Well, that's my cue."

"Thanks for my oatmeal."

"No problem. Call me if you need anything while I'm out."

"I will-"

"I wanna holla at you after work, Playboy, so don't leave," Dante blatantly interrupts.

"Gotcha."

Velour rolls her eyes at Dante before turning back to Freeman.

She displays a sweet-tasting smile that sends his hormones straight to orbit.

"Catch you later."

"Okay."

Again, Freeman pries himself from her bedroom eyes to double-time it toward the stairwell.

Freeman must have checked his seatbelt a dozen times to make sure it was secure because the way Dante is barreling down First Avenue, one would think he was competing in a NASCAR event. But you cannot steal a man's joy when his every wish has finally been granted. Still, he would love nothing more than to read his friend's approved bid notification without being jolted uncontrollably on the ride.

"See, this is the reason why my mother's gone; because of this shit right here," Freeman blares out. "Slow it down a little-"

"My bad, dawg." Dante slows his Nissan Armada down to eighty. "What's it been, three months? I can't imagine what you and Dee's been going through, but y'all seem to be holding up pretty well-"

"We're managing, alright? Don't get it twisted." Freeman finally focuses on the form. "So next Saturday is it, huh?"

"Yes! And I'll be officially out of that god-damn station!" Dante shouts in glee while beating on the steering wheel. "I swear, Free, this couldn't have come at a better time—trust me when I say that!"

Freeman glances over at his overjoyed coworker who is bobbing his head to Johnny Gill's *Rub You The Right Way*. Never can he recall in his two-year tenure seeing this low-fade haircut wearing, Bronx native this animated nor this loud. The proud father of two boys and a committed husband of eleven years to his sweetheart, Daphne, tends to successfully keep his private life away from everybody at the station. Even when he occasionally hangs out with the crew, except for laughing at each passing joke that would fly by, Dante never has too much to say about anything.

Lately, the only time anyone would know that he even has a pulse is when he and Velour get into their epic battles, and aside from those, at times, getting really ugly, he would make some of the funniest remarks anyone has ever heard. It is a shame nobody from Midway will ever catch a glimpse of his true personality. Freeman, on the other hand, gets a front-row seat to Dante's hidden dramatic side, as they converse about his sudden departure.

Freeman hands him back the form. "But you never mentioned parcel post before."

Dante mashes his horn at a slow-walking teenager giving him the finger.

"THE FUCK OUT THE WAY THEN, STUPID!" Dante calms back down. "I put in for it like a year ago, but I didn't want to make a big deal about it, you know what I mean? Folks always wanna stay in your business. *Uh, why you wanna go over there?* Cuz I want to, that's why! Nosy bastards!"

Freeman silently gasps at every turn Dante barely makes. "Got tired of the letter carrier role, huh?"

"Man, you just don't know. I'ma tell ya...it had gotten to the point where I was really thinking about quitting the whole system. Just up and leave and never look back!"

Freeman wonders if the whole Velour ordeal influenced his friend to consider that option. "For real?"

"For real, yo. But now since I have THIS!" Dante holds up his notification form like the Statue of Liberty holds her torch. "I know I'll be alright from here on out. I love driving trucks, man. You're basically your own boss. You don't have anyone all up in your grill every minute of the day, asking you stupid shit. You don't have to depend on anybody but you. You feel me?"

It's Velour.

"I understand that, trust me. I feel that most of us, well the guys anyway, would take a truck position over pushing that cart any day."

"True dat." A sly grin appears on Dante's face. "But now that I have THIS!" He shows Freeman the form again. "My departure will allow a certain someone to take my spot on the route, making that girl the happiest person in Midway."

Freeman chuckles. "So, we got jokes now..."

"What she be saying about me, bruh? Y'all be having them long-ass lunch dates not for her to mention about the goings-on of our route. What's up?"

"C'mon man, you know how you two are."

"I know, but I want to hear her version of it."

Knowing that Dante is going to keep pressing the issue, Freeman says, "A'ight, let me put it to you like this; she knows y'all weren't meant to be paired up. Aside from that, she did say you're a hard-working individual and a cool guy deep down." Freeman pauses for a moment. "...but you're also pigheaded."

Dante almost sideswiped a parked bus from laughing so hard.

Freeman grips the seat's armrest in fright.

"*Pigheaded?*" Dante shrieks. "Aww, man...that's okay, though. All I know is when they post that position up for bid next week, you will be the perfect partner for Velour."

"Well, actually, I was thinking about putting in for the truck assignment I'm on now—"

"Shiiiiiiit." Dante cracks up. "My man; you are not getting that truck assignment, you can forget that! Ain't it up for bid right now?"

"Yeah, and I put my name down, Jordan signed up and if I'm not mistaken, Jose must've put his name on the list today—"

"And Jose is going to get it because he has more seniority than you and Jordan put together, you know that."

"Yeah, I guess," Freeman mumbles, in partial defeat. "But I was kind of hoping-"

"You better *hope* your ass is on my route before they ship you to another station! And I know you don't want to go anywhere else, especially since ole girl would be missing the hell out of your ass! She digs you, bruh, I mean *really* digs you! That's all I hear her talk about when she's on her phone yapping to her cousin. *Freeman this, Freeman that.* And don't get me wrong, she's the bomb-diggy, but I don't need to tell you that, right? You better put in for my route, Playa."

Freeman vaguely hears the last part. He is still replaying, "*...she really digs you...*" inside his head.

"I'll give it some thought."

"What is there to think about? You've been on my route, you know how sweet it is—nice, clean buildings with doormen who take all the parcels and sign for all the valuable mail...big-ass mailboxes in ninety-five percent of my buildings. I've updated the names in all the mailboxes. My route book is up to date–what more do you want?"

"I know I don't want to be transferred, that's for sure." Freeman adjusts himself in the seat. "I kind of like the atmosphere at Midway."

"Well, then you know what you have to do." Dante merges onto the free-flowing FDR Drive Highway. "And you know homegirl is going to do her best to recruit you, so that's icing on the cake."

Freeman blushes while gazing out the window.

"Did you hit it yet?"
Freeman snaps his head back around. "What?"
"You heard me!" Dante smirks. "I SAID, DID YOU HIT THAT YET?"
"What is up with everybody?" Freeman tries to conceal his smile. "Velour and I are just cool peeps! What, I can't be friends with a fellow coworker?"
"First of all, she's not a fellow, let's be clear on that! Like you haven't noticed all that meat she's packing in her uniform pants?"
"Now, I didn't say I was blind, either…"
"You better act like you know! Shoot, you could hook a train up to her caboose and be like, ALL ABOARD! CHOO-CHOOOOO! YOU KNOW WHAT I'M SAYING? She got a big ole badunk-a-dunk!"
Freeman laughs. "You stupid, man…"
"You know I speaks the truth! And she's waiting for you, my brother…what you gonna do? CHOO-CHOOOOO! RIDE THAT PONY! THAT'S WHAT YOU'RE GONNA DO!"
They laugh hysterically while cruising down the frigid FDR Drive, en route to the boogie-down Bronx.

Freeman steps inside of his co-op apartment and heads straight to the kitchen to place his groceries on the counter. He kicks off his work boots to avoid tracking any dirty ice into his carpeted living room area. After peeling off the rest of his uniform, leaving only his tank top and boxers on, he closes his eyes and then cocks his head back. He stands idle for a moment to allow his six-foot-one, semi-muscular, dark-complexioned frame to soak in all the welcoming heat that is simmering inside his domain; a meditating ritual he does every day, regardless of the season.
He then slides on his flip-flops and returns to the kitchen to retrieve the smaller brown bag he brought in along with the groceries. From the bag, he pulls out a pint of E&J (the liquor

store did not have his Hennessy for some reason) and twists off the cap to take a quick swig.

Ahhhhh.

Lastly, he grabs another small greasy bag with the shrimp rolls and drags his tired body into his living room.

Before collapsing on his sofa, he presses the button on his answering machine to hear two messages he received. The first message brings a smile to his face.

It's from his pops.

"Hey, Freeman. It's me. Just calling to see how you're making out. I'd kind of made a big dinner by accident; some baked chicken, with cabbage and rice, smothered in gravy–your favorite. You can stop by and help me and your sister woof it down if you haven't eaten yet. Give me a call back."

Freeman stops smiling when the second message plays.

"Hey baby it's me, um, I guess you're not at home, gimme a call as soon as you get home. I called you earlier this morning and left a message on your voice—"

Freeman erases the message before he can hear the end of it.

Stretched on his couch, he takes bites of his dinner and heavy gulps of his liquid comforter. He fondly remembers how Lovelle would come in and decorate his apartment to her liking, adding a different, yet unique signature of her in each room. That was four months ago when feminine aromas such as perfume, hairspray, and potpourri reigned dominant. After she packed up and left, the manly and undesirable odors of feet, Lysol, Chinese food, and liquor mixtures quickly returned and settled in. He often wonders what he could have done differently to have avoided such a nasty falling out with the woman that he's been involved with for a little over ten years. And this shift in the relationship occurred a week after his mom's sudden death.

When it rains, it definitely pours.

The first thing he must do at this point is to stop being evasive with Lovelle because she is now obsessed with planning a wedding within the year—something which he feels is not going to happen. The "let's-work-it-out" plan is not working out at all; at least not on his end, and the relationship is feeling like more of a chore at this rate. He had better clear things up real soon because it won't be long before he invites Velour over to his place for some *milk-n-cookies*, and that would not be fair to either one of them. Then, as far as the job, there is the possibility of getting shipped to another station if he does not put his bid in for something permanent at Midway.

Just too many decisions at one time.

He takes a long swig of his drink, then another, and another, allowing the creamy contents to calmly guide him to a deep state of abyss until morning.

LORRAINE

*L*orraine rushes inside the house and quickly shuts the door to block the evening's treacherous winds which are forcibly trying to follow her inside. Dropping her bags on a nearby bench, she examines her frigid face in the bronze sunflower adorned mirror as she pulls off her full-length chocolate mink coat. After fluffing out the curly ends of her long mane, she snatches off her brown high heels, wearily advances into her living room area, and plonks down onto her plush leather couch to let out a long sigh of relief. She immediately grabs her foot to massage.

I'm getting too old for this vain crap.

But when the mother of two beautiful young women is constantly mistaken for their older sister, vanity gets engrained in her, after a while. If anything, she wishes she still had their stamina, as this January will mark fourteen years for her as a real estate broker, and physically it is beginning to take its toll. Her feet have taken such a beating in the heels that she chooses to wear when she is showcasing properties to her clients. At this point, however, she needs to invest in a pair of comfortable walking shoes—*fashionable* walking shoes, of course.

The delightful aroma of a home-cooked meal invades her nostrils. Now she no longer needs to order out like she initially planned because, as usual, Cadina has saved the day.

"YOU GOT THE HOUSE SMELLING GOOD, CADDY!" she yells toward the kitchen.

"HEY, MA!" a tired voice responds.

Lorraine forces herself up from the couch, returns to the foyer, grabs one of the bags, and sashays into the kitchen where her youngest daughter is holding a skillet of cornbread with an oven mitt. "What do I smell up in here, girl?"

Cadina places the pan on the stovetop. "I made barbeque turkey wings with honey garlic ginger, collard greens, yams, and of course, the cornbread. Something quick...gotta big day ahead of me tomorrow."

That statement echoes through Lorraine's head like church bells. She pours herself some apple juice and then leans against the island to watch her daughter as she fixes her plate.

Sipping on her juice, Lorraine recalls the earlier period of her life when she began prepping her, then teenage girls, to be able to know their way around the kitchen. While her oldest daughter, Camille, stuck to the very basics and became a highly regarded hair salon owner, (*My man loves my hair, not my meatloaf!* she would laugh.), Cadina grew quite fond of 'banging the pots and pans'. Over the course of time, she raised her newfound skills to newer, exciting heights by enrolling in the world-renowned Institute of Culinary Education and receiving her associate degree in Culinary Arts. To this day, she still cuts out recipes from the back of Ebony and Essence magazines to add to her culinary repertoire. Whoever spoke about food had Cadina's attention, hands down.

But unfortunately, her attention span fell short in other areas, such as holding down steady employment. Over the span of six years, she has had a total of nine jobs that she just couldn't hold onto. Three of those jobs did lay her off, but five of them she left because of lack of interest. The last one she had, did not even last a month because they fired her. That shocked everybody because not only did her father's friend hook her up with the position; it was in a popular soul food restaurant located in Harlem which provided her the opportunity to utilize her skills as a cook. Cadina never told anybody why they let her go. However, the head chef/

owner told Lorraine that he had an argument with Cadina over food preparation.

She wanted to do things *her* way.

Several warnings later, the owner released her. That dismissal did not sit well with Lorraine nor her husband—at all. Now she has been given, what her father calls, one last chance. Maybe things will turn out better this time. Who knows? Then again, maybe Cadina will find a way to toss this job to the curb like all the others. Lorraine hopes not because her husband had to pull some major strings to get her a position at the post office. *Major* strings. And if Cadina ever finds it in her mind to deliberately insult her daddy again by following her free-spirited mindset, she may as well leave town.

Cadina hands her the steaming plate of piping-hot edibles.

"Thanks."

"You're quite welcome." Cadina grabs herself a seat at the dinner table. "How was work?"

Lorraine sits down and quickly blesses her food before replying, "Child, just long. Had this one couple who had the nerve to catch an attitude with one of my agents, simply because she refused to show them a two-bedroom apartment...but they have *nine* kids and another on the way."

Cadina chuckles. "You're lying..."

"I tried telling her that these landlords are not going for that. So, she got offended and they stormed out of my office. Like I said—long day."

"Shoot, the struggle is definitely real," Cadina says, letting out a yawn. "The way rent is skyrocketing in this city, it's literally impossible to live comfortably unless you *and* your other half both have two good jobs-"

"*Ohhh.*" Lorraine injects. "So, this means you're going to act like you *need* this job your father went out of his way to secure for you, right?"

Cadina darts her half-sleepy eyes at her mother. "Noooo, I'm not planning on botching up this gig, Ma. I know this is a career opportunity and I've thanked him numerous times, so I don't see why you feel the need to go there-"

"Because I *can*, that's why. Don't act like we don't know how you operate." Lorraine takes another sip before positioning her body to face her daughter. "First, you quit the banking position last year. *I* hired you, but you weren't feeling the real estate industry, so you left that, but then you get released from a place we thought for sure was right up your alley-"

"Look, I know I messed up big time at the restaurant; Dad grills me every chance he gets, so the last thing I need is for you to co-sign his guilt trip, please? Not tonight?"

Lorraine reads the pleading in her daughter's eyes and decides to let it rest for the time being. She then reaches alongside her seat for the bag that she brought into the kitchen and hands it to her daughter.

Cadina gives her mother a suspicious smile as she pulls the shoebox from the bag and opens the box top. She pulls out a pair of black Reebok Cross-Trainers and then tries to conceal her obvious appreciation.

"Maaa, now you know you didn't have to," she squeals, with one foot already in a boot.

"And that was the last pair they had." Lorraine chuckles at the fact that she's the reason her daughters are spoiled to the core. "Consider it a token of my love."

The phone rings.

With both boots on, Cadina jumps up, gives her mother a fat "thank you" kiss on her forehead, and then reads the caller ID before pressing the talk button on the handset. "Hey, Daddy... Nothing much, just admiring my first-day-on-the-job gift mommy bought for me...Some boots." Looking at her mother, Cadina asks, "He wants to know if they're postal-regulated?"

"Yes, they are," she replies between munches. "Where's he?"

"She said, *yes*. Where are you now? Okay, I'll tell her. Love you more, bye." She hangs up. "He's on his way home."

"Are you going to crash here tonight?"

"Yes, I bought my things. Wish me luck tomorrow."

Lorraine cocks her eye at her slim, yet curvaceous, brown-skinned daughter with the long, jet-black ponytail. With a straight face, she says, "Honey, I usually do a lot more than just wish."

Cadina grants her mother a fake smile before walking out of the kitchen.

Lorraine returns to her meal, all the while saying a prayer to herself on Cadina's behalf.

And for her and her husband's sanity.

CADINA WILSON

*a*fter a soothing shower, Cadina tiptoes into her bedroom to finish drying off her damp body. She then sits at the bottom of the bed, and as she lotions her legs, she glances around her room which is filled with timeless memoirs of a well-rounded, if not privileged past–Portraits of her from different periods of her life hug the walls with quiet reflection, right along with posters of her favorite musical artists: the Force MD's, Stephanie Mills, Earth, Wind & Fire, and LL Cool J. Collectible items from various New York exhibitions are neatly displayed on each dresser and nightstand, highlighted by her favorite piece, the steel metal replica of the Empire State Building, which reaches a good two feet in height. Autographed photos of BellBivDevoe and other Summer Jam headliners are either framed or tucked firmly in each corner of her vanity mirror, reminding her of the days when she and Camille used to run rampant to every concert that came within the tri-state area. There wasn't a wasted opportunity in a household where parents provided infinite possibilities of enjoyment and fulfillment. Each day was an event, the next day was greater than the last and the summers were adventures all by themselves. As long as she and her sister kept grades of A's and B's, their childhood expeditions would never be shortchanged.

But just like Miss Jackson would sing:
Funny...How...Time....Flies.......

The more she drifts down memory lane, the angrier she becomes at herself. Placing the cap on the lotion, she pauses in frustration. While her big sister continues to make a name for herself in the salon industry, Cadina still has the nerve to be running around like an irresponsible groupie. Living in a self-absorbed bubble for so long, she has unintentionally managed to make a mockery of the very people that she loves and respects the most. That whole restaurant disaster was the straw that damn near broke her daddy's back. Never in her entire life had she seen him so angry. And with good reason. He felt it was a slap in the face for all that he tries to do for her.

Still, he somehow managed to find her employment within the postal system. Now, that's either unconditional love from her father, or he is on a hell-bent mission to turn her into an independent woman.

Her phone rings.

It is Camille.

Cadina answers the phone and places it on speaker while slipping into her pajamas. "Whazzuuup…"

"Whazzuuup!" her sister greets. "Just calling to check up on ya."

"I'm good. Still at your shop?"

"Girl, yeah. Trying to finish up on my last customer so I can close up, but she ain't trying to go home!" Camille lets out a hearty laugh through the phone. "Ready for your big day tomorrow?"

Cadina lay across her bed on her stomach. "I guess. Nervous, though."

"You'll be fine."

"Daddy threatened to disown me if I screwed this one up."

"After what you did at that restaurant, I don't blame him one bit."

"What?"

"Look, we understand that you graduated with a culinary degree, okay? But who on God's green earth told you it was a good idea to create your own appetizers behind the owner's back? It was not your place to make those decisions."

"Wow. And all this time, I thought you were my ride-or-die sis-"

"I am, but sometimes you have to swallow your pride and own up to your mistakes, Boo."

Cadina rolls her eyes, but then a thought crosses her mind. "You think I'm cut out for this postal gig?"

"As long as you deliver mail to the right address...I mean, besides that, how hard can the job be?"

Cadina ponders. "I know, right? Thanks, Cam."

"Get some rest and call me tomorrow. Love you."

"Love you more."

Cadina turns off her phone and plugs it into the wall charger. She walks over to her vanity mirror and pulls out a picture–a photo of her with her daddy, taken by her mother at graduation. She is proudly displaying her culinary degree. The smile that her father displays is filled with pride. As she studies her father's face, with its hints of Cherokee blending in with strong African American features, it's as if she can hear him lecturing her through the six-year-old pic:

Playtime is over, baby girl—time to grow the hell up!

Another yawn escapes her as she returns the picture and climbs into bed.

Determined not to disappoint her parents again, she says her prayers and makes the promise to the Almighty Himself, as the soft seduction of the Sandman's whisper lure her closer to a world better known as a brand-new day.

THE CREW

"*A*hhhh, yeah. That's that Rick James shit right there…" Cycle Floater Letter Carrier Louis Rodriguez nods his head as the classic *Cold-Blooded* instrumental beat from his boom-box slices through the quiet morning that blankets Midway Postal Station's loading dock area. With eyes closed behind his black-rimmed glasses, one can sense that the cocky Puerto Rican from Bedford-Stuyvesant, Brooklyn is about to go into full concert mode.

Forced to witness this b-boy routine are drivers and crewmembers Roy, Neville, and Shabbazz, whose purpose at this very moment is to constructively critique Lou's untested rhyming skills before he shares them with the entire hip hop world. A dream he has been longing to do for many years but has now decided to put into action.

The Latino lyricist opens his eyes wide and begins his performance…

"Lou is what? Sexy, Sexy, Sexy Sexy…
But he's known to be, COLD—BLOOOOOOODED!
The industry is over-flooded,
Infatuated with cats with mumble raps,
The Psycho Floata, Party Promota coulda told ya,
I didn't come to throw bricks, son, I rip boulders,
I can't help but to spit fire that reaches full throttle,
Ricocheting through your heart from shots that's primed hollow,
Never lacking in confidence, I cherish my own bravado,
Trust me when I say I'ma hard act to follow,"

"—Excuse me—"

"*Cuz Lou is what? Sexy sexy sexy.... Baby girl come test me,
Fulfilled her kinky needs with this potent Latin breed,
Papi Chullo has juice flowing from his floppy seed,
I'ma thief in the night, you might consider it a felony,
A midnight marauder while your broad is taking care of me,*"

"—Uh, excuse me?—"

"*Bitch keeps telling me, I pack more than Ron Jeremy,
She brought her flock over and we created group therapy,
But the stimulation factor doesn't happen in my chapter,
I want them hoes that can freak it just by hanging from the rafters—*"

"EXCUSE MEEEEEE!"
"WHAT THE FUCK, MAN!"

A ticked-off Lou turns around to see who has the audacity to cut his cipher short. The lanky Latino turns off his radio and joins the rest of the crew as they silently gawk over the person who has just walked up the loading dock's ramp.

Standing in front of them holding a folder and wearing a black leather jacket over a red hoodie, black jeans, a pair of Reebok Cross-Trainers, black earmuffs, and a nervous smile is a beautiful sista who stops waving at them now that she has caught their attention.

"Oh, sorry to bother y'all," she says. "...but is there another way inside your building? The front entrance is locked."

"We don't open 'til eight, Ma," quips Lou. "Come back in a half-hour."

"No, see, um, I'm supposed to meet up with Mrs. Tucker, I think she's the assistant manager. I'm Cadina Wilson."

Roy, the muscular Albino, bumps past Lou to speak to the new arrival. "You're the new sub, right? Forgive us, we didn't know. Welcome aboard. My name is Roy. This is Big Country right here..."

"A.K.A. Neville, at your service," The squatty driver greets, shaking her hand.

"My man, Shabbazz..."

The dreadlocked driver shakes Cadina's hand. "Pleasure meeting you."

Lou greets Cadina with a straight face. "They call me Lou, Da Psycho Floata, Rip-A-Party Promota—holla at your boy."

"Oh, uh, okay." Cadina politely grins at Lou.

"Don't pay him no mind." Roy points through the glass door. "Look, you go through this door, then the other door and walk all the way down towards the back and the manager's office will be on the right, she should be in there."

Cadina repeats the directions to herself. "Okay, thanks a lot. Nice to meet y'all."

"Likewise," they chant in unison.

The crew watches her walk through the main employee entrance before running over to the door to catch another glimpse of the new ponytailed employee as she makes her way down the corridor. When she enters the manager's office, they turn to each other with delighted approval.

"Now *that's* whuzzup!" Neville confirms, smelling the perfume Cadina left on his hand.

"Oh, no doubt," Roy agrees. "*And* she has a mean bow-legged walk, too? *Whew...*"

Shabbazz grabs his hand truck and states, "Fifty bucks says she won't make it past probation."

"Damn, son, she just got here!" Roy twists his face at the dreadlocked driver. "How you gonna say some evil shit like that?"

"You saw the way she was holding her folder...like she was cuddling a teddy bear. I just don't see it in her-"

"Hell, *your* ass almost didn't pass probation, you forgot about that?"

"Yeah, because they put me on that bullshit route that Dee is on right now," counters Shabbazz, locking his hand truck inside the cargo area of his postal truck and closing the door. "I was coming back to the station damn near every night-"

"Yo, fuck all that! I wasn't finished spittin'!" Lou stares at his comrades like they lost their minds. "So, what's up? Y'all feeling my joint or what?"

Neville and Shabbazz zip up their parkas and board their trucks, leaving Roy to become the unlikely spokesman. "Yo, we'll talk later, a'ight?"

Roy turns around, jumps off the dock's ledge, and then hops in his truck.

Still standing in the same spot, Lou shouts at his boys through revved-up truck engines and exhaustion. "A'IGHT! THAT'S HOW Y'ALL GONNA BE? COOL! IT'S ALL GOOD, BABY! WE'RE GONNA BE DOING A WHOLE LOTTA TALKING—"

But his tantrum goes unheard as, one by one, the three trucks roar out of the loading dock area and down the street in clouds of smoke to start the morning collections.

Alone in his funk, the aspiring rapper gathers himself, grabs his boom-box, yells out to no one in particular, "NEVER LACKING IN CONFIDENCE, BABY! Damn, it's colder than a mufu out here...", and runs into the station to start casing his route for the day's delivery.

CADINA

*C*adina makes a right as told by one of the drivers. She sees an office with the door ajar and light conversation spilling out.
Must be this one...
Entering the office, she spots a lady behind a desk talking on the phone. Judging by the lady's tone, it sounds more like a personal call.
Cadina pulls off her ear-muffs and quietly takes in the award-heavy room, where achievements the station has garnered over the years hang honorably on the four walls that surround her. Her eyes land upon an oil-painted portrait of the manager-in-charge. A bald, dark-skinned man in a dark-blue suit sitting proudly behind his desk with his hands clasped together and the American flag flanked behind him. What captures her attention is the man's eyes; so self-assured, so confident, so commanding—
So intimidating.
The lady holds up a finger to motion that she is about to wrap up her conversation. "No? Well, look behind the microwave... See, now the next time you won't fling your keys on the counter with so much force as you did last night...Another long day, probably...Alright, talk to you later, love you, bye." The lady hangs up the phone and then shakes her head with a smile. "Why my perfectionist of a husband struggles to find his keys every morning is beyond me."
Cadina flashes a new-to-the-job smile.
The assistant manager rises, showing her 'WNBA-type' height while her autumn-colored, cable-sized dreads rest against her long, lean back. She extends her hand to Cadina.

"I'm Mrs. Denise Tucker, the assistant manager of Midway station. You must be Cadina Wilson, right?"

Cadina winces at the unexpected strength the skinny lady possesses. "Yes, I am."

"Welcome aboard—now follow me, please."

Before Cadina can say anything, the tall manager grabs a couple of manila envelopes that were on the desk and power-walks out of the office. Cadina plays catch-up along the way.

"The first thing we must do is get you squared away on the truck."

Cadina suddenly stops. "Y-You putting me behind the wheel already?"

Tucker spins around, causing her beige buttoned-down jacket and matching skirt to flow like a matador's cape. "Well, not exactly. One of my drivers is going to train you on various assignments. It's vital you learn the truck position as soon as possible because that will be one of your duties for a while, in addition to actually delivering the mail, okay?"

Cadina deadpans, "I guess."

Tucker laughs. "Child, you'll be fine. And you'll be in good hands with Freeman Souls. He'll be your trainer for the entire week."

Cadina follows Tucker up the stairs and onto the second floor where Tucker is immediately motioned over by an impatient supervisor.

Tucker sighs, "As soon as I step foot on this floor, people claw for my assistance. Miss Wilson, do me a favor and go see the man at that podium. His name is Mr. Chapman. He'll be your immediate supervisor in Section C. And tell him I'll be right over for further briefing."

"Mr. Chapman, right?"

Too late...Tucker is already en route to her supervisor.

Taking a deep breath, Cadina begins making tracks down the work floor to her newly assigned section. As she unzips her jacket, she feels the eyes of employees all over her. She smiles nervously at some of the younger male carriers who huddle up quickly to evaluate 'the new kid on the block', while the older carriers take a brief look at the new face and return to their breakfast or their phone.

The closer she gets to the section, the more her eyes soak in; like the convoy of blue mailcarts lined up along the many route-cases that zigzag throughout certain sections. And everywhere she looks, there is mail—on the floor, on huge skids, in steel-caged post cons, leaning next to route-cases, magazine bundles on top of magazine bundles colliding with oversized priority packages, and letters overstuffed in long plastic trays.

This is her new home.

Cadina feels tired already.

She makes her way to the podium where Supervisor David Chapman is bending down over a stack of mail and scribbling on his clipboard.

The sandy-hair Irish supervisor in a brown tweed coat and brown loafers straightens up to greet her. "Cadina Wilson, right? I'm David Chapman, Section C Supervisor. Welcome aboard."

"Nice to meet you and thanks."

Mrs. Tucker arrives, glancing at her watch. "Have you heard from Freeman, David?"

Chapman smiles at Cadina. "Will you excuse us, Miss Wilson?"

Cadina nods as Chapman and Tucker veer off to the side to talk privately. But she still manages to eavesdrop on their conversation. She keeps her eyes on them.

Chapman drops the smile. "Freeman called in sick...again. Saw his name on the call-in sheet."

Tucker frowns with her arms crossed. "This is getting old, David."

"This marks, what, the third time he's called out in the past two weeks?"

"Ever since his mother's passing, he's been more off than on around here," mutters Tucker. "A line needs to be drawn because I'm not tolerating any more absences from him."

"Well, now I'll have to pull somebody off their route to get his truck from the garage and start his run which will be two hours behind schedule-"

"No. Have someone go and bring his truck back to the station and that's it," Tucker orders. "I'll get another carrier from the other section to do his relays but in the meantime, have Roy, Neville, or Shabbazz split up Freeman's collection-run and morning-drops. That should minimize the damage."

"And I can put the new kid with Lexington to get her familiar with his route before he leaves the station, altogether."

Tucker nods in approval. "When Freeman shows up tomorrow, tell him I want to see him in my office first thing."

"Will do."

They break up their meeting.

Cadina pretends she was not eavesdropping on their conversation as they approach her.

Tucker says, "Change of plans, Miss Wilson. Mr. Chapman will get you situated from this point on, okay? Best of luck to you and again, welcome aboard."

"Thank you," Cadina responds as the assistant manager marches down the work floor.

Chapman turns to Cadina. "Come with me, Miss Wilson."

While following the supervisor, Cadina glances at her new coworkers. She walks by a petite dark-skinned carrier sporting a Halle Berry hairstyle, who seems aggravated as she sorts the mail. She stifles a chuckle as she, once again, sees the Puerto Rican carrier named Lou, who is bobbing his head to some music playing in his headphones as he cases the mail. And then her eyes land upon an attractive light-skinned carrier with blond hair and a high-powered physique, who apparently has been watching her the entire time. The attractive sista smiles and waves at her. Cadina waves back.

They reach their destination and Chapman gains the attention of a male carrier who is writing something down in a ledger. The carrier peeks up at Chapman, but immediately his eyes divert to Cadina. The carrier straightens up and turns his body towards them, never letting his eyes off her.

Then the carrier smiles.

It was the creepiest smile Cadina's ever seen in her life.

"Lexington, I would like for you to meet Cadina Wilson," Chapman states before turning his attention to her. "Lexington will be leaving soon for the Supervisor's Academy, so this will become your temporary assignment, in addition to training on the truck during your probation period."

Cadina extends her hand. "Nice meeting you."

Lexington reaches for her hand. "The pleasure is *all* mine."

The moment their hands touch, Cadina absorbs all the wrong vibes from this guy who continues to blatantly probe her body with his beady eyes while bits of saliva pack the corners of his mouth.

Plus, he is getting a little too comfortable with holding her hand.

She politely snatches her hand from his slimy grip.

"I trust you will train her properly?" Chapman asks Lexington.

"I'll teach her everything she needs to know," Lexington assures, before turning his perverted eyes towards Cadina. "You can count on it."

She feels violated.

"Great!" Chapman shakes Lexington's hand and turns back to Cadina. "We'll postpone the truck assignment til tomorrow morning. Any questions, don't hesitate to ask, okay?"

"Yes, Sir."

"I'll check on you later."

Chapman pats Cadina on the back and returns to the podium.

Lexington rolls up his uniform sleeves, claps his hands together, and rubs them vigorously. "Ready to get this party started?"

She gazes at all the mail in his workstation. "I guess so."

"Have you ever worked in this type of environment before?"

"No, I haven't."

"It can be very fast-paced." He picks up a tray of letters and plops it on the route-case ledge. "The goal is to case the mail, then break it all down so you can go out and deliver to businesses and residential buildings and return back in a timely manner. And that's it. Nothing complicated at all. And I'm going to break down everything you need to know about this route."

"Gotcha." She hangs her jacket on a coat rack and then rolls up her sweater sleeves. "What do you need me to do?"

That repulsive grin returns to Lexington's face. "I like that."

She cautiously asks, "You like what?"

He folds his arms like an emperor. "The fact that you're ready to get down to business. And that's what this station needs; more hard workers like you. We have enough slackers around here who act like they can't grasp that concept. They feel as if cutting corners is the way to go and that's why the post office's name is continuously dragged in the mud. But hey, no need to dwell on any negativity, right?" Lexington sneers.

She raises her eyebrows. "Okay..."

He grabs a handful of letters. "Now, I'm going to be throwing around a lot of postal jargon so bear with me, I'll break them down as we move along." He takes a deep breath and grins proudly. "This is what we call casing or sorting the mail, which basically means placing the mail in the slots with the matching address and apartment number, okay? Now, we start with the first-class letters, then the large envelopes and magazines which we call flats and end with the bulk mail." He then says to himself, "*Yeah, I'ma get you good and ready for my route...*"

Cadina patiently listens, all the while wishing she had a piece of mint to offer him.

Three hours have passed, and her gut instincts were right.
She is going to have problems with this dude.
Although he tries to come off friendly, she sees the nasty disposition Lexington possesses just by the little things he does early on–things like launching letter trays on the ledge which miss her arms by mere inches; trying to boss over people, such as an old mail-handler who distributes the mail to various workstations. She can tell that the old man dislikes coming over to Lexington's workstation because of how this arrogant fool snatches the mail from his hands and scolds him for stacking the mail the wrong way. Then, Lexington occasionally turns around to say something sarcastic on the sly about how she is casing the mail. However, nothing infuriates her more than how this nincompoop feels the need to get all up in her face to say something, giving her the impression that he wants to kiss her. At one point, she has no choice but to politely check his behind. This slightly offends him, but he gets the message. Now that the mail has been cased up, she wants the day to hurry so that she no longer has to be in his 'self-absorbed' presence.

"So, what do we do now?" she asks, pushing up her sweater sleeves.

"Well, we wait to see if there is more mail arriving to the station," he explains, with his chest puffed out and his arms crossed. "Normally, you would take care of your return-to-sender mail and forwardable mail like I did while you were casing up those magazines. Now, remember to always check the hot case every half hour for loose mail, even right before you leave the station, alright? And always remember to case up your first-class letters before you case up anything else, then your second-class envelopes and magazines, then your bulk mail, and please remember that you do not case up the DPS mail, which is short for delivery point sequence mail since it's already in order—"

Cadina watches Lexington do about three double-takes at Lou, whose workstation is across from his. With his headphones blasting, the Latino carrier dances and sings to himself while closing his relay bags and throwing them on the relay skid next to him.

"*Teh-leeee-foooo-noooo...suena, suena, suena, suena, suena, Teh-leeee-foooo-nooooo...penas, penas, penas, penas, penas...*"

Lou does a couple of two-step moves before he loads up another bag of mail, causing Cadina to chuckle. Unfortunately, she notices Lexington, who is not finding it amusing at all.

"Excuse me for a moment," mutters Lexington.

He squirms his way between relay skids and steps over a couple of empty letter trays to tap his dancing coworker on the shoulder.

By the way Lou spins around and rips off his headphones, Cadina gets the feeling he does not appreciate Lexington killing his salsa mood.

"What?" barks Lou.

"What you mean '*what*'? You and your loud singing and dancing—that's what! Can't you see I'm training a new sub over here?"

"First of all, you're not supervising today, Papa, so don't bring that bullshit over here-"

"I don't have to be supervising to tell you that your little sideshow act is becoming a major distraction-"

"Are you *serious*? How am I disrupting you from *way* over here, huh?"

"Do I need to call Davenport up here to tell you to tone it down? Because I will if you—"

"YO, TAKE YOUR NON-SUPERVISING ASS BACK TO YOUR ROUTE AND LEAVE ME THE HELL ALONE! I DO THE SAME SHIT EVERY DAY, BUT NOW SINCE WE HAVE A CUTIE UP HERE, YOU WANNA GET ALL BOUGIE AND SHOW YOUR ASS! BUT I GOT

NEWS FOR YOU—YOU COULD KISS MY GOYA ASS TWICE! YOU HAVE NO BUSINESS IN MY SPACE, PAPA!"

"OOOOOOOOOOOOOOOOO!"

An embarrassed Lexington peeks around to see the other carriers laughing. He turns back to Lou. "You're ignorant, you know that? I can't even talk to you like a mature adult-"

"Fuck outta here, man." Lou returns to loading his relay bags while making it his business to sing even louder. "TEEH-LEEE-FOOO-NOOOOO...."

The entire section sings in unison, "SUENA, SUENA, SUENA, SUENA, SUENA-"

"ALRIGHT, SECTION C, KNOCK IT OFF!" yells Chapman, returning to the section. "THAT'S IT FOR THE MAIL! LET'S TIE DOWN AND HIT THE STREETS!"

Cadina watches Lexington retrace his steps back to his workstation.

"We're going to start tying down the route now," he says in a low, aggravated tone. He points to the panel on the top. "Start from up here."

"Okay." Cadina begins to place rubber bands around the mail bundles.

"And after we finish tying down, we'll go downstairs to get our arrow keys, scanners, and our valuable mail, which consists of certified mail, registered mail, and Express Mail." Lexington then grumbles under his breath, "*I'll be glad when I get the hell outta this station.*"

Cadina tries hard not to laugh as she prepares her bags for her very first mail delivery.

Pushing their mailcarts through the side entrance of the first stop of their day, a mid-century architectural-styled Co-op on the corner of Eighth Street and Fifth Avenue located in the Greenwich Village area, Cadina follows her trainer into the well-maintained lobby area. Her eyeballs bounce from one wealthy tenant to another, who is either leaving through the revolving doors or rushing in from the cold and waiting on the elevators.

Lexington shouts, *"VINNY, WHAZZUP?"*, to the young Italian doorman wearing a red jacket and sitting behind the front desk, who in return, peeks up at Lexington, and gives him the finger before returning to his phone.

"He always plays around like that," Lexington says.

Cadina rolls her eyes.

They swerve around a circled desk with their carts into a spacious, well-lit room where fourteen silver mailbox panels stretch across three walls, and a large oakwood island nestled in the center. They peel off their jackets and begin grabbing numbered mail bundles from their carts to place in front of its designated panel.

"You start over on that end, and I'll start over here and we'll work our way towards the middle," Lexington orders.

Cadina, promising herself to say as little to this guy as possible, does as told.

An hour passes and she struggles with finding names inside the mailboxes while Lexington, on the other hand, zips through each panel on the opposite end and slams the panel doors to emphasize a point he made earlier en route to the building:

I'm the fastest carrier at Midway!

What a way to start off her first day, with this type of nonsense. Even when she asks him about letters that do not have an apartment number, he brushes her off by commanding her to *just put them off to the side and I'll get to them after I finish;* like she's bothering him, while he makes it his business to kiss every tenant's ass that walks into the mailroom.

A distinguished-looking gentleman wearing a puffy ski jacket strolls in and opens his mailbox which is next to Lexington.

"PAUL! HOW'RE YOU DOING, MAN?"

Lexington shouts so loudly that Cadina could have sworn the poor man jumped an inch off the tile floor.

"Oh, uh, I'm doing just fine," Paul politely replies, while retrieving his mail from the box. He strains his eyes as he points at Lexington. "It's Lenny, isn't it?"

"C'mon, you know my name...*Lexington*," he says with a stupid grin. "You're funny, Paul!"

"Oh, I see you're training a new person..."

"Yeah, she's a cutie, isn't she?"

Cadina stops immediately and faces the smiling fool.

Flipping through his letters, Paul pulls one out and hands it to Lexington. "This one's not mine, I think it belongs to the other Williams guy in 4-B."

He takes the letter, examines it, and then reaches it out to her. "Here, it goes in 4-B."

You put it where it belongs, Mister Flash—you're the one who did it!

She ignores him while working her panel.

"Never mind, I'll handle it." Lexington tosses it onto the island and turns back to Paul, who is now leaving the mailroom. "Hey, Paul! I didn't see you this past Christmas. Did you have a nice holiday?"

Turning around, Paul displays a huge phony grin. "It was wonderful, Lenny-"

"It's Lexington-"

"I'm sorry...*Lexington*. I took the family to Aspen!"

"Really? How was it?"

"Beautiful! It was my daughter's first time. Now she thinks I'm the coolest person, next to Chris Brown, of course-"

"That's nice, that's really nice." Lexington nods while rubbing his sweaty palms together. "Because I didn't get a chance to *see* you before the holidays, you know..."

"Ohhh, right, I totally forgot about you, didn't I?"

From the corner of her eye, Cadina watches Paul dig deep into one of his corduroy pants pockets and pull out a thick wad of cash. He flips a crisp hundred-dollar bill over, then another hundred over, then a fifty.

She peeks at Lexington, who waits patiently.

Damn near salivating.

Paul finally flips over to a wrinkled five-dollar bill. He pulls it out and hands it to Lexington, who accepts the shabby-looking bill with a stupid look on his face.

She fights hard to conceal her laughter.

"I'll remember to stick it in a Christmas card the next time, Lenny," Paul says, patting Lexington on the shoulder. "Keep up the good work…and train your new coworker well!"

"It's *Lexington*," he mumbles, but, by now, Paul has already left the mailroom.

Fighting hard to keep a straight face, Cadina grabs a batch of the letters without apartment numbers and walks over to Lexington. "These are the ones whose names I couldn't find inside any of the boxes—"

He snatches the letters from her hand and storms over to the panels where she had been working.

Oh, no he did not snatch those letters outta my hands-

That was it.

She's had about enough of this guy's rude behavior and decides to confront him.

"Lexington, I need to have a word with you" …but, she cuts herself off in mid-sentence.

Cadina stands motionless as she listens to Lexington grumble to himself while shoving the letters inside the correct boxes.

"'Keep up the good work,' he says. Yeah, I go above and beyond the call of duty every day, ALL DAY, but you can't break a brutha off better than a five-spot? What am I supposed to do with that? Buy bubblegum? You could've kept that raggedy bill… stingy bastard!"

He slams the panel door so hard that she feels the rattling sensation vibrating through her bones. He turns around to face her and in a surprisingly calm manner says, "Were you about to ask me something? I didn't mean to cut you off-"

"Uh, nooo, you're good." She decides it is best not to say anything to this crazy-ass coworker of hers until he is in a better place emotionally–and mentally.

"Okay. I believe we're done here." He grabs a mail bundle from the island. "I'll be back, I'm going to leave this with the doorman. You did good in this building, Cadina."

She acknowledges the compliment, all the while, watching him stare at her with that Grinch-like smirk she is beginning to loathe. But as he smiles, he also balls up the wrinkled five-dollar bill and flings it into a wastebasket that's underneath the island before he heads to the front desk.

She begins to collect the rubber bands and the return-to-sender mail from the island to place them back into her pushcart. Then she bends down to retrieve the five-dollar bill from the waste bucket, stuffs it in her pocket, and waits patiently for her looney trainer to return.

Three o'clock rolls around with Cadina and Lexington returning to the station. She pushes her mailcart at the speed of light down the slick sidewalk, trying her best to distance herself from her yapping trainer. But he matches her speed, stride for stride. On and on, he babbles about himself, dulling her senses. And now he is asking questions pertaining to her personal life.

God, why'd you do this to me?

"What did you say you used to do before coming to the p.o.?" he asks.

She cuts her eyes at him. "I said I worked at a restaurant for a while and decided to leave."

"What made you leave?"

"I dunno. Just left."

He grins. "I see you're not really big on conversation."

"It's not that, but could you do me a favor?" She stops walking and faces Lexington, who stops pushing his cart, as well. "Ease up on the flattery when we're amongst people? It's kind of embarrassing and I didn't appreciate that remark you made to that tenant earlier-"

"My bad, Cadina," he apologizes. "I saw it on your face and definitely didn't mean any harm by it."

"Thank you."

They resume pushing their carts down the sidewalk.

"But don't act like you don't warrant that kind of attention," he adds. "I was merely stating the obvious-"

"Lexington, just behave. Alright?"

His pompous smile shines on his face. "Lexington is now behaving himself."

Cadina shakes her head.

As trainer and pupil turn the corner en route to the station's loading dock, they bump into Mrs. Tucker. Right behind her is the person Cadina saw earlier in the oil painting—Mr. Davenport. Even buried underneath his wool coat and Baldwin hat, she can feel his commanding presence. When she shakes his hand, she feels herself becoming paralyzed by his dark, glowing eyes, and his outrageous smile.

"Did I just talk her up or what?" Davenport gleefully says to a smiling Tucker. "I was just telling Denise that my day was about to close, and I didn't get a chance to meet our new employee! Cadina Wilson, I'm Michael Davenport, the manager-in-charge; welcome to Midway, and how was your first day of delivery?"

"I-It was good," Cadina stutters.

Davenport's eyes intensify. "He talked you to death, didn't he?"

Cadina's hesitancy causes everyone to laugh.

"Now I wasn't that bad, was I?" Lexington asks.

"Oh, you *are* a talker," Cadina confirms. "Don't act like you're not."

"Well, I'm glad your first day here was a positive one." Davenport pats Lexington's shoulder. "You mind if we have a moment with the future supervisor?"

"No, go right ahead."

The managers huddle up with Lexington on the corner.

Cadina pushes her cart toward the loading dock ramp and waits until they are done with their prized pupil.

"Hey, newbie! Welcome home!" greets a couple of senior letter carriers, leaving the station for the day.

Cadina smiles while waving at them.

Her eyes just happen to gaze across the street.

And the sight she sees causes her to scoff under her breath.

No, he did not show up at my job...

Leaning on his black 2013 Cadillac CTS Coupe with his arms folded is a tall suave-looking man wearing a black wool trench over a black suit. With black shades covering his strong African American and Cherokee features, the gentleman with the cool Malcolm-X fade smiles at her. She simply shakes her head. The man glides across the street with his trench coat flapping in the cold wind and gives her a warm embrace. He is known to the world as Vernon, but she simply calls him daddy.

Cadina takes off her father's shades and hands them to him. "I see you didn't waste any time."

"Actually, I was on my way to buy a new laptop."

"But you just so happened to make a pit-stop to check up on me, right?"

Vernon's sculptured smile says it all. "Somewhat."

Lexington pushes his cart towards the ramp and then joins in on the conversation. "How're you doing, Sir."

Cadina smirks at Lexington and says, "Daddy, this is my instructor for the week, Lenny VanGuard—"

"The name is *Lexington* VanGuard, Sir." Lexington cuts his eyes at Cadina. "And I'm proud to report that your daughter is learning rather quickly for her first day on the job."

Vernon stares at Cadina. "Don't let up on her, young man."

She twists her face.

"I won't let you down, Sir." That Grinch-like grin returns to Lexington's mug as Cadina hands him the certified letter receipts. "I'll see you upstairs."

Lexington pushes his cart up the ramp and onto the elevator lift.

Cadina shudders. "Of all the people they could've paired me with, my supervisor chooses that looney-tune to train me."

Breathing on his sunglasses, and then wiping them off, Vernon asks, "Oh, really?"

"Oh really, what?"

"Well, it appears to me that no matter where you wind up, you seem to have issues with management. You tell me who's the common denominator in all of this?"

"Are you going to make this a daily routine? Swinging by the station to evaluate my every move?" She pauses and peers down the street to maintain her composure. "I think I've learned my lesson from that whole restaurant disaster, so there's no need to babysit me, okay, Daddy? I can handle this job."

Vernon slides his shades back on, turns around, and without looking back at his daughter, says, "Finish up so we can go get my laptop."

Cadina watches her father return to his vehicle. She mutters to herself and then rushes her mailcart up the ramp to enter the open elevator lift. As she waits for the gate to close, she pulls off her earmuffs and makes a mental note to bring her earbuds tomorrow—just in case she is paired up with Lexington again. She hopes this is not the case, for this will be the ultimate test of her patience. Worse, it could also determine her fate in keeping her promise to her parents.

The gate finally closes, just like her unappealing first day at her brand-new job.

FREEMAN

*F*reeman stumbles through his apartment door with the force of a clumsy bull and throws his groceries onto a kitchen chair. Pulling off his snorkel jacket, his eyes dart around the kitchen area and the realization hits him—it has been cleaned up. All the dishes have been washed and put away. The counter is clear from opened cans and cereal boxes.

He slowly enters the living room and continues to scan his surroundings. Chinese food containers are gone, rug vacuumed, pillows fluffed, and properly placed back on the sofa and recliner. He takes a couple of whiffs in the air.

Potpourri?

Damn.

Freeman grumbles to himself as Lovelle Taylor steps out of the bathroom and approaches him to plant a kiss on his lips. Never breaking stride, the chocolate-skinned lady, still dressed in a beige cardigan sweater draped over a white dressy blouse and brown-pinstripe flare-legged pants covering up brown boots, walks over and sprays leather cleaner all over the couch and recliner.

"One of these days, you're going to wake up and find a roach crawling inside your mouth; this place stays a hot mess." Lovelle pushes the vacuum into the closet. "Sink full of dishes, food containers all over the place, Chinese rice in and under the sofas, and it *stinks* in here! But are you going to change your ways? Probably not."

"You paint a lovely picture, Bee-Bee."

The elementary school teacher, with the full bob hairdo that covers one of her slanted eyes, stares at him. "I haven't heard you call me that in a while."

His original pet-name for his fiancée was Bee-Bee, short for "Brown Buffy", on account of her plus-sized frame. Lovelle, on the other hand, despised her lifelong weight problem. Thanks to Shaun T's DVDs and a strict low-carb diet, she rigorously pushed herself into losing the sixty pounds she marked as her goal in less than two years and remarkably succeeded. Now "Brown Buffy" transformed into "Tootsie Roll" which became his second pet name for her. Suddenly, Lovelle, sixty-three pounds lighter and beautifully toned, began to exude the self-confidence that she never had in her younger years.

On one hand, he applauded her efforts, for he could not imagine anyone *not* putting an extra pep in their step after accomplishing such a huge personal goal. But on the other hand, it came with a heavy price.

"It has been a minute, right?" Freeman recalls while pulling off his hoodie. "Thought you were getting your workout on at the gym."

"I went this morning before work. Heading to choir practice in a few."

"So…how was school?"

Lovelle, who continues to clean, drags a heavy garbage bag next to her, and says, "Well, aside from Antonio bouncing off the walls because he forgot to take his medication again, the other kids were actually on their best behavior for a change, so I had a good day."

"That's good." He forces a smile as falls back in the recliner to untie his Timberland boots.

"I wanted to stop by and see how you were doing and if you needed anything, but it's obvious you're feeling much better."

"Why wouldn't I be?"

"Well, according to your sister, you caught a stomach virus this morning."

He peeks up at her, confusingly. Then it dawned on him about the lie he told Divine earlier that morning on why he did not make it to work today.

"Oh, yeah... *Yeah*." Freeman sits up to embellish on the untruth. "Came outta nowhere. But I went to the bathroom a few times, flushed it right on out. Feeling much better now-"

"Really..."

She digs into the garbage bag and pulls out an empty bottle of Hennessy and holds it high for him to see.

He twists his lips and returns to unlacing his boots.

"So, I guess this cured that little virus of yours, huh?" she asks, but not waiting on a response. "Or was this the actual *virus* that made you miss another day of work?"

He pulls off one boot. "I'm not in the mood for one of your little lectures, Lovelle-"

"Freeman, either you let me schedule you an appointment with a counselor or at least talk to Pastor about your obvious drinking problem-"

"I don't want to talk to your *father* and I damn sure don't want you making any appointments for me. Why? Because I don't have a drinking problem!" He yanks the other boot off with so much force, it goes airborne. "Let this be the last conversation we have about this-"

"Well, if you don't want to hear my mouth, then I suggest you start throwing away these empty bottles I keep finding underneath your bed-"

"Maybe there's a reason why I like to have a taste every now and again. Ever took that into account?"

She fixes her lips to say something, stifles it immediately, and places the bottle back inside the bag.

He knew that would shut her up.

She then walks over to retrieve her purse, which was laying on an end table. Eyeing her every move, he observes her digging into her purse for something. She returns to him with a forced smile.

He remembers when her smiles were infectious glows of light that used to make him feel like he was sitting on the moon, looking down at the world. These days, her smiles are filled with hope. Hoping to recapture that unbreakable union they once shared so deeply because everything now seems so off-kilter.

Kisses are now bitter.

Touches are cold and awkward.

Conversations strained and pointless.

He knows it has been her strength alone that has been keeping the relationship afloat this far. It is only a matter of time before he finds a way to just let it go, but for now, the charade drags on.

"I didn't come over here to argue with you." She opens his hand and places two tickets in it. "You remember that musical at the Palace Theatre, *Holler If Ya Hear Me*, you said you wouldn't mind seeing? Well, two tickets for next Saturday, front row at eight o'clock."

He studies the tickets for a moment and then tries to hand them back to her. "Nah, take one of your homegirls. Hell, take Dee, she digs stuff like this."

"Freeman..." She ignores the tickets as she stares at him, baffled. "You were very adamant about going to see it before-"

"That was then, this is now. I don't want to go see it-"

"You know what? This is crazy. This, this whole thing is just crazy!"

She takes a deep breath to regain her composure. She then sits on the recliner's armrest, next to Freeman. "Are you sure you're ready for this?"

"Ready for what?"

"The *wedding, married life*, you know what I'm talking about. It's less than six months away-"

"How many times are you going to ask me the same question?"

"Until you give me an honest answer-"

"That rock on your finger ain't enough for you?"

"But that was the extent of it!" She strains to keep her voice at an even keel. "You act like you never have time to sit down with me and talk about how many people we're inviting to our wedding. We haven't even settled on a color nor a particular theme-"

"We're sitting down right now," he affirms with a blasé tone. "Cancel choir practice and let's talk-"

"No, no, see, this is what I'm talking about. You don't seem to be the least bit excited about any of this and I'm sick and tired of having to track you down just to have this conversation. The last thing I want is the both of us wasting each other's time because I'll tell you right now, I could focus my energy elsewhere-"

"Yeah, well, we all have our options now, don't we?"

She glares at him. "And what does that mean?"

"It means, I'm tired and I'm hungry. If you want to talk about the wedding, fine, let's talk. If not, don't be late for choir practice."

He reclines in the chair and grabs the remote from the end table.

Lovelle shoots him a *'I can't believe you're acting like this..."* look before grabbing her purse and heading to the closet to retrieve her coat.

"You forgot these."

He extends the tickets towards her.

She thrusts her arms through the sleeves and then buttons her coat, all in a heated fashion. "Like I said, I bought them for you. And the next time we have a conversation, Freeman, at least *act* like you care about what the hell we're talking about. Alright? Have a good night."

Lovelle storms out the front door.

Freeman sighs as he tosses the tickets on the end table. He straightens the recliner and trudges towards the kitchen. He grabs a small bag and pulls out a pint of E & J Brandy, the apple flavor. He quickly screws off the top and downs a big gulp. He wipes his mouth and then turns his attention to a photo magnetized to the refrigerator. A year-old memory of him and Lovelle hugging each other and acting goofy at a skating rink.

A happier moment in time.

Seems like centuries ago.

He takes another swig, grabs another bag, which contains Jamaican food, and trudges back to the living room to watch some television.

The phone rings.

He checks the caller I.D. to see if it is Lovelle, deciding to give him a piece of her mind after his smart remark. Instead, it is a number that brings a smile to his face. He wipes his hands before touching the handset.

"Hey Velour, I didn't expect to hear from you until tomorrow… Nothing, just sitting here, about to watch a little tele…" Freeman belts out loud laughter. "Nooooo! Not another Dante episode! What happened now?"

Rejuvenated and liquored up, Freeman's conversation with Velour, along with the E & J Apple Brandy, is finished precisely at two o'clock in the morning.

The screaming phone jolts Freeman out of a deep sleep. He reaches to get the handset from the floor and then presses the talk button. Grogginess takes hostage of his voice. "H-H-Hello?"

"The hell with '*Hello*'!" Roy yells on the other end. "You know what time it is?"

Freeman rubs his eyes to focus on the clock on the cable box—6:05 am. He yanks the covers from his body and springs up from the sofa. "Shit! Where you at?"

"At the garage, staring at your truck without you in it. This is getting old, Free."

"Shit! Shit!" is all he can mumble as a sharp pain detonates inside his head, causing him to double over in agony.

"Yo, I went ahead and fueled your truck and loaded the back with empty tubs and buckets, so the only thing this truck needs is *you*."

Freeman struggles to slip into the only decent uniform he can find. His head is pounding with the force of a sledgehammer. His eyes are blurred from interrupted sleep. *Lord, help me get through this day!* "Yo, I owe you big time, man–"

"Fuck all that! Just get your ass here, Tucker is pissed!"

"Wh-What she say–"

Roy hangs up on him.

After lacing up his dusty boots, he sits on the edge of the sofa waiting for the room to stop spinning. As his drunken world continues its carousel, mournful images of his mother's funeral are summoned from his subconscious.

His heavy eyes begin to close.

Other images follow suit, such as he and Lovelle racing against one another on rollerblades throughout Flushing Meadow Park in Queens.

He begins to drift away.

The final image is Mrs. Tucker on the phone leaving him a brutal message on his answering machine.

His eyes pop open like a surprised owl.

Throbbing head and all, Freeman grabs his postal parka, his hat, and staggers out of the apartment.

"Nights like this, I wish, that raindrops would fall..." echoes around Freeman's brain, along with streams of pain that blast off like roman candles. The agony causes him to swerve his truck from side to side all the way down Third Avenue.

As he makes a right on Eleventh Street, he has already accepted the fact that today is going to be one of those days. He's already had to absorb a vicious tongue-lashing from the cab driver for puking in the back seat of his car, so the last thing he needs is Tucker and her verbal heat chastising him.

He pulls up behind Roy's postal truck which is parked in front of Webster Hall. He turns off the engine and sits there for a moment to sober up.

Roy hops out of his truck and trots over to see Freeman slumped over the steering wheel. "Yo, for a minute, I didn't think you were gonna make it here on time."

"I didn't, either." Freeman pushes himself off the steering wheel, steps out of the truck, and welcomes the fresh, freezing air. "Yo, I appreciate this, man—"

"WHOA, SON!" Roy repels a few feet from him, holding his nose. "I know you're going upstairs smelling like ass! And Tucker's upstairs waiting on you, too! You better go gargle and throw on some cologne. Shoot, *gargle* some cologne, do something!"

Roy's advice falls on deaf ears as Freeman beelines it through the employee entrance, stumbles up the staircase, and then pauses for a second to allow the queasy feeling in his stomach to pass before he speed-walks the rest of the way to his section, and finds Tucker and Chapman standing at the podium.

The assistant manager and supervisor trade glances, giving Freeman the impression that they do not like what they see. Freeman checks his appearance. *Shit.* His uniform shirt buttons are not aligned with the holes, plus his shirttail is sticking out of his zipper. Tucker's eyes are about as dark as the two-piece pantsuit she is wearing.

"Walk with me over to the timeclock," Tucker orders through clenched teeth.

Feeling more agitated than embarrassed, he snatches off his beanie, rubs his hand through his afro, and glances at his nosy coworkers, who are watching the play-by-play drama unfold at the podium.

"NOW, FREEMAN!"

He drags his body over to the timeclock where Tucker stands with arms folded.

"Haven't I spoken to you about this matter before?" she asks.

He tilts his head to brave a sharp pain. "Yes, you have, Ma'am."

"But yet, you're not comprehending. Look at you! You come waltzing up in here late and looking like a hot mess–"

"What difference does it make now, Mrs. Tucker? I'm here, right? Who am I training?"

He watches Tucker swing over to an attractive lady with a long ponytail, wearing an orange hoodie, and staring at him like he has lost his mind.

"Miss Wilson, help the mail-handler give out the mail, and then report over to Lexington's route, thank you."

The new sub slips on her gloves and mumbles to herself before assisting the elderly mail-handler.

"I know what you're thinking, but I'm really okay!" Freeman states. "You see I drove the truck over here without any problems, so you don't have to make a big deal out of this—"

"Don't you dare tell me what I need to be doing, Mr. Souls, who do you think you are?"

"Look, if you don't want me to train the new sub, can I at least do my collection run without all the drama?"

Tucker turns to Chapman. "Are all of our drivers gone?"

Chapman checks his watch. "About an hour ago. And the transporter truck will be here soon to pick up the early collection mail." Chapman leans closer to Tucker and in a low voice, advises, "I know what you're thinking, Denise, and if I were you, I wouldn't have him on the road in the condition he's in-"

"But I'm telling you both I'm fine," Freeman desperately reiterates between yawns. "Just let me do my job, that's all I ask."

Tucker glares at him, pondering a critical decision. She then moves closer to his face and whispers, "When you are finished with your collection, you don't do anything else except report to my office—do I make myself clear?"

"Crystal."

Freeman spins around and marches down the work floor. He feels the weight of everybody's eyes on him, which prompts his legs to nearly trot to the stairwell. As he does, he almost collides with Velour, who stops short of him with two steaming cups in her hands.

"Hey," she says, scanning Freeman up and down. "Are you okay, Baby?"

Her voice, as soothing as aromatherapy, sobers him up just a bit.

"I'm good. Just in a rush, that's all."

"I caught you at the right time. I knew we were going to pay for all of that talking we did last night so I went ahead and bought you this. It's your favorite, French vanilla espresso."

She hands him the toasty cup. He gulps on the espresso feverishly.

"This was much needed, thanks."

"I know you gotta run, our boss is eyeballing us as we speak."

"So what else is new?"

She caresses his hand. "You need anything else from me?"

That was a loaded question, and she knows it.

"I'm good…for now."

"Call me if you do."

She gives him another long, knowing stare before letting go of his hand.

His eyes gravitate to the hypnotic sway of her hip-hugging postal pants walking away.

In his line of vision, he also captures Tucker, who is monitoring his every move. She gestures with a pointed finger, making it loud and clear-

Why are you still here? Get To Work!

He snaps out of Velour's bootylicious spell and spirals down the staircase.

Freeman barrels through his morning collection run at a torrid pace. After every mailbox he empties, he makes sure he scans it, and then slams the door with enough force to wake up the entire village area. As his hangover fades away, frustration takes its place. Never has he disrespected anybody the way he did Tucker, who, by his own admittance, has been very patient with him and his personal drama. But that is all about to come to a crashing halt. The scales have been tipped by his smart mouth and whatever Tucker has waiting for him in that office will be justified because of his dumb actions. Freeman shakes his head in shame. His moms taught him better than that.

He parks in front of his last collection box on Cooper Union. He hops out, opens the mailbox, and shovels all the mail into his bag. From the corner of his eye, he notices a lady flagging down a taxi a few feet in front of his truck. That reminds him to bum some money from Divine until he can get to the ATM. His vomiting inside of the taxi that morning was costly, and it caused him to shell out an extra twenty, the last he had in his wallet, which went towards tipping and cleaning.

After throwing the bag into his truck, he slides behind the wheel and pulls out slowly to swing around the taxi.

In a split second, the taxi, unaware of Freeman passing by him, begins to bolt off.

"What the..."

Freeman bangs on his horn, but it was too late.

BAM!

"Oh, no...No...NOOOOO!"

He slaps the gear in park and flies from the truck to see the rear right side of his truck and the front left side of the taxi crushed against one another.

"*Stupid muuufucka, man!*" he screams in outrage.

Hopping out from the passenger side of the vehicle, the skinny cab driver raises his fist at Freeman with equal fury. "What the hell is wrong with you? You didn't see me pulling off? Are you blind?"

"Am *I* blind? You slammed into *me*, idiot! Jesus, I can't believe this shit!"

The driver quickly sizes up Freeman and senses victory in his favor. "You drunk! I smell it all over you! Ohhh, you in big trouble, your company is paying for this!"

This is not happening, it can't be happening!

Freeman stands with his hands on the top of his head in disbelief. When he sees the cab driver pull out his cell phone and storm off to the side, panic grips in, and Freeman frantically digs his phone out of his pocket to call the station. Chapman is going to have a fit. And that would be peaches and cream compared to what Tucker might have in store for him. He was right all along.

It was going to be one of those days.

DENISE TUCKER

*R*ocking back and forth on the podium's chair, Tucker monitors Chapman's section while he investigates Freeman's accident. As carriers approach her with loose mail they've received from the hot case, she jots down the count and smiles. But deep inside, she is a nervous wreck, blaming herself for allowing Freeman to drive a company vehicle under the condition he was in. He could have killed somebody or himself for that matter. All because she was more concerned about having the collection mail ready for the transport truck rather than her own employee's wellness. Her body shudders, causing her to spill a little coffee on her blazer.

The intercom blares out her name.

"MRS. TUCKER, YOU HAVE A CALL ON LINE TWO. MRS. TUCKER, LINE TWO, PLEASE."

She lunges for the phone, almost knocking the base to the floor. "Midway Station, Tucker speaking."

"Shouldn't that be Assistant Manager Tucker or are you still having trouble grasping that esteemed accolade?"

If there is one person other than her husband that can make her smile in a time of distress is her longtime friend, Dexter Whitehead. Both started out as letter carriers in the late nineties before becoming supervisors at the same post office in the Bronx and then branching off into different fields within the postal system. She has not heard from him in almost a year but after hearing his baritone voice, she can still visualize the portly little man with bulging eyes standing flat-footed in front of her.

"Dexter, I'm going to slap you the next time I see you! How're you doing?"

"I'm doing just grand. Now, tell me why I'm hearing about your promotion through a third party?"

"My apologies, Dexter. Been swamped with paperwork, learning my new position, you know how that goes. What about you? You still supervising at Cooper Station?"

"Well, no. Actually, I've been supervising over at VMF for the past eight months."

VMF?

He's the Vehicle Maintenance Facility Supervisor, which means he must be at the scene where Freeman and Chapman are to investigate the accident.

Tucker's smile drops from her face.

"Okay Dex, lay it on me; how does it look?" She asks, holding her breath.

"Well, I've seen worse. I don't know if you were aware of it, but your supervisor allowed your driver to operate a vehicle, despite his condition—"

"I allowed him to resume his duties, Dexter, it was my call."

"But, *why*? You put this man in an extremely dangerous position. This is not like you-"

"I know, I know." Tucker rubs her forehead. "If we weren't so short-staffed around here, things would've been different—" She cuts herself short to avoid making any excuses. "I take full responsibility for his actions."

"Be grateful. The accident wasn't his fault. The other driver smacked into the back of the truck, plus his license was suspended, so that clears Freeman of any violation."

"Thank God." Tucker exhales. "I promise you; this won't ever happen again."

"I know it won't. Starting tomorrow, he is prohibited from driving any company vehicle for at least a year. I don't care if he's the only employee you have left in the building. Understood?"

"Yes."

"Now, as a friend, I'm going to omit that part from my report. But I strongly suggest you send a stern message to your driver regarding his condition and the horrible repercussions it could have led to–follow me?"

"I owe you big time, Dex."

"And you can start by treating me and Pearl to a bowling match. And tell your husband to bring his A-game with him."

"Will do and thanks so much. Bye."

Tucker hangs up the phone. The trembling in her hand flares up again as her emotions try to get the best of her. She takes a couple of deep breaths.

Relax, relate, release…

She vows not to let Freeman and his personal baggage drive her to a sudden demotion or to an early grave, whichever would come first. She has too many personalities to deal with at this station to focus on just one. No, this time around, she is going to deliver the kind of ultimatum that is going to send an unexpected jolt into Freeman's diluted reality.

But first things first. She must figure out if she is going to tell Davenport the whole truth behind Freeman's unfortunate incident or handle it her way.

In her mind, she has no choice but to choose the latter, or she'll risk looking like what Davenport describes as an incompetent individual who is unprepared to make critical decisions, let alone run a station.

Regaining control of her bearings, Tucker takes Freeman's badge, walks over to the time clock, ends his day with a single swipe, turns around, and roars at the top of her lungs, *"BREAKTIME, EVERYBODY!"*

CADINA

*a*t the sound of the assistant manager's thunderous voice, Cadina hurries to finish passing out the final letter trays located inside the caged post-con. She picks up a tray, reads the label, and approaches Velour's workstation where she finds the statuesque bombshell sitting on a stool, quietly eating a cup of oatmeal, and flipping through an Ebony magazine.

"Hey," Cadina greets. "Where do you want me to put this?"

"You can slide it right under here, that would be fine."

Velour scoots over to allow Cadina room to slide the tray underneath the letter case. When she stands back up, Cadina quickly sizes up her glamorous coworker–a flawless-complexion, light honey-skin woman, sporting a blond Farrah-flipped hairdo. She's donning a super-tight postal shirt that generates significant attention around the bosom area. No stomach to be found over her belt and hips curved to perfection. And Cadina had already taken notice of the booming derriere Velour is blessed with. By and large, the quintessential hourglass figure that every man dreams of sporting proudly by his side.

"Thanks," Velour replies, with a tropical smile.

"No problem."

Cadina begins to walk away.

"Now, if I see you pick up another tray of mail during breaktime, girl, I'm going to scream. You hear me?"

Cadina turns around. They both break into laughter.

The diva-carrier extends her hand. "Velour Patterns—welcome aboard."

"Thanks. Cadina, uh, Wilson." She shakes Velour's hand. "Excuse my nervousness—"

"Please," Velour casually dismisses. "We all get the willies on our first week at work. Shoot, I just don't want to see you pick up another tray while you're on break."

"I don't mind, really. I only have two more trays left in that cart, and then I'll chill for a minute—"

"Allow me to school you, Newbie." Velour holds up her hand to motion for silence. "First and foremost; always and I do mean *always*, take your breaks and your lunches. Trust me, when you're out on your own delivering the mail, you're going to value those breathers, okay? Now, repeat what I just said. Come on now, I don't hear you…"

Cadina laughs. "Okay, okay! I promise to take my breaks and my lunches."

"You better. I'll be watching you."

Something or *someone* catches Velour's attention, causing the diva to smile.

"I see someone's back from vacation."

Cadina turns her head to see who she is referring to.

That is when her jaw drops, and her eyes widen.

Making their way towards the section are two letter carriers: an older white gentleman and a black gentleman.

A very *handsome* black gentleman, at that.

Cadina stares at the brother with thirsty intentions.

The two men wrap up their conversation and the older gentleman veers off, heading to the supervisor's podium. The handsome brother remains on course to Velour's workstation.

She wipes the gawky expression from her face and says "Hi" to him as he approaches. He politely greets her and then continues forward to greet Velour.

"James is in the building!" Velour announces as she gives him a warm hug. "How was vacation?"

"It seems like I was never on one." He places his shoulder bag down and peels out of his postal jacket. He then motions to Cadina. "New sub?"

Velour turns to her. "Cadina Wilson, meet James Richards, one of the coolest brothers to ever deliver the mail."

James chuckles as he shakes her hand. "I don't know about all that, but welcome aboard."

As she shakes his firm grip, she can barely look at this five-foot-nine, caramel-colored, thick eye-browed, juicy lip specimen, without blushing. But her poker face remains intact. "Thank you."

"Alright, James," Velour says, with pending excitement. "You know what I'm about to ask you, so let's hear it..."

He locks his arm out and shows off a set of keys. "Me and Moms move in next week!"

"That's what's up! Congratulations, Mr. Homeowner!"

Velour slaps James a high-five and he pumps his fist in the air, further exemplifying his elation.

"Thanks. I'm so glad this week is over. Dealing with the loan officer and home inspectors, stressing my ass out! But I'm happy my moms can finally move out of her apartment, so this is a beautiful moment."

"Awwww," both ladies chime in admiration, and they began to laugh.

"That is sooo nice," she says.

"Thank you, Cadina." James stares into her eyes. "That's a unique name, I like it."

"Why, thank you. I'll tell my parents you approve of it."

"You do that."

They both smile at each other.

"I know a housewarming is in the works, right?" Velour asks.

"I'm already on it."

"Good. Cuz I need to go somewhere and look cute. You know how we do, right, girl?"

Cadina laughs. "You are crazy."

"BREAKTIME IS OVER LADIES AND GENTLEMEN!" Tucker blares from the podium. "LET'S GET BACK TO WORK! Miss Wilson, come to the desk, please?"

"Okay!" Cadina turns to Velour and James. "That's my cue. Talk to y'all later."

"Alright," they simultaneously respond and resume their conversation.

Cadina approaches the podium. "Yes, Ma'am?"

"This way, please."

She follows Tucker over to the older letter carrier's workstation. The tall man with the ghoulish-looking eyes behind a pair of thick bifocals does a double-take at them both.

"How're you feeling this morning?" Tucker asks.

"Fine," the carrier grimaces while organizing his area. "I placed my ninety-six form over on the desk for an hour of overtime, that's all I'm going to need to finish up today."

"I have the form right here." Tucker holds it up to show him. She then turns to Cadina and says, "Miss Wilson, this is Marc Speid, our senior carrier at Midway. Marc, this is Cadina Wilson, our new sub."

Cadina sticks out her hand. "Nice to meet you, Sir."

After running his fingers through his buzz-sawed military-style haircut, Marc straightens his pocket-pen protector, adjusts his thick glasses, stares at Cadina without shaking her hand, and finally glares at Tucker. "What's this all about, Denise?"

"I read the doctor's note you threw on my desk this morning stating that you're fit for duty and while that may be true, I'm going to have Miss Wilson assist you at the end of your route-"

"If I wanted somebody to help me, Denise, I would've requested it," the old-timer counters. "I'll be just fine-"

"Look Marc, I really don't feel like debating you on this one. Do I have to remind you about the brief encounter you experienced last week?"

"My medication had to be adjusted, Denise." A tempered expression arises on Marc's face. "That was the problem all along. Trust me, I feel a hundred percent now-"

"Miss Wilson is going to assist you and that's final-" Tucker finds herself raising her voice, so she quickly pulls back. "I want you to retire next year in one piece, okay? Please, it's been a long morning already."

Marc grumbles as he resumes his work.

Tucker turns around to depart from his workstation. Cadina follows suit.

When they return to the podium, Tucker turns to her. "Don't let the mean look fool you, he's a teddy bear, trust me. Now, Chapman has you assisting Lexington and once you're done, you'll pivot over to assist Marc on his route. Any questions?"

"So, I won't be training on the truck today?"

"In due time." Tucker smiles. "Continue handing out the mail, please, thank you."

The assistant manager grabs a manila envelope from the podium and marches down the work floor.

Cadina slips on her gloves to pick up a tray of letters. She takes a couple of steps and then stops. She does a slow three-hundred-and-sixty-degree turn to soak up the busy scene occurring at her new job. Almost all the carriers are either talking amongst each other or singing and dancing in their own private worlds, but the one thing they have in common is that they are casing their mail at phenomenal paces. And she can see why.

It seems as if the mail never stops coming.

Cadina snaps out of her trance and scurries over to a workstation to hand a carrier his letter tray. When she turns around, she catches James peeking at her, as he continues to converse with Velour.

Picking up another tray of letters, she keeps her poker face intact, but her insides tingle with glee.

Two-thirty in the afternoon and Cadina pushes her mailcart down Sixth Street. Her face feels like a thick sheet of ice due to the frigid wind whipping around in the area. She doesn't mind one bit. She will take this over the company of Lexington any day.

She arrives at the corner of Sixth Street and Second Avenue. She pulls out her arrow key to unlock the two large green relay boxes on Marc's route. She opens the first one; nothing is in it. She opens the second one...same thing; empty.

Puzzled, she pulls out a form from her coat pocket to make sure she is at the right location. She reads the form and the street signs twice before confirming to herself that everything is correct.

A lady in a two-piece business suit rushes out of a garden apartment, waving a couple of letters in the air. "I'm so glad I caught you. Could you take these for me, please? I'm in a hurry."

A blank expression appears on Cadina's face. "Huh?"

The businesswoman quickly withdraws her mail. "You *are* the mail-lady, right?"

"Uh, yeah, I'm the mail-lady, but what do you want me to do with those?"

"*Excuse* me?"

"I'll take them off your hands, Mrs. Baker."

Cadina turns around.

Marc Spied pulls up and accepts the mail from the businesswoman.

"Thank you, Marc," the businesswoman says, while slowly backpedaling. "She must be new."

Cadina notices a stark difference in Marc's demeanor as compared to the attitude he displayed when she was introduced to him earlier.

There is actually a *twinkle* in his ghoulish-looking eyes.

"She's a motivated prospect with a bright future ahead of her," he states with a rugged smile.

"Well, she looks scared to me." The businesswoman slides into her running BMW. She shouts to Cadina, "No worries, dear, Marc will get you right! Tah-Tah!", before she pulls off down the street.

The senior letter carrier lets out a hearty laugh before speaking. "You better get used to people handing you mail and asking for directions; that's Carrier 101."

Cadina cracks a smile, welcoming his jovial spirit. "Gotcha. But wasn't I supposed to deliver your last block? I looked inside the relay boxes, but didn't see any bags in them-"

Marc shows her a couple of empty bags in his hand and then stuffs them back inside of his pushcart. "I trust you won't tell anyone." he winks.

Cadina shakes her head. "Marc...now you know I have to get familiar with my position before my training period ends. That's the only way I'm going to build my speed up."

The senior carrier snatches off his thick glasses and wipes them clean, all the while, maintaining a mischievous grin. "I totally understand."

He slides his glasses back on and then digs into his postal shoulder bag. He whips out a vintage postal winter trooper cap, still in its package.

"You need this more than me."

He rips the plastic open, walks over to take off her earmuffs, and places the furry cap on Cadina's head. "There. Now you're official, at least from the neck up."

Adjusting the hat and blushing, she says, "Thanks, but you didn't have to—"

Marc waves her off. "Ah, it's a token of my apology regarding my behavior this morning. And it's one of the original winter caps from back in *my* day. I bought it off eBay, mind you, so it wasn't cheap. Wear it in good health." He turns his mailcart around, preparing to leave.

"I will." She stuffs her earmuffs in her pocket. "Now what am I supposed to do in the meantime?"

Pushing his cart down the street, Marc yells, "Did you eat yet?"
"Well, no, I was about to—"
"Go eat!"
Marc points to a little 'hole-in-the-wall' restaurant called The Stage across the street.
Might as well.
As she waits for the light, she glimpses at the senior carrier slipping and sliding down the street at the speed of light, especially for a man his age.
"I want you to retire next year in one piece!" That is what Tucker said to the old-timer.
But denial can be a mutha, Cadina muses.
The light turns green.
Cadina crosses the street, heading straight to the restaurant for some welcomed heat.

Sitting at the counter, Cadina sips on a hot chocolate with marshmallows. She evaluates her second day on the job. She was supposed to be trained on the truck, but that did not happen because her driving instructor appeared to be dealing with a massive hangover. She met a cutie by the name of James, who seems to have *his* eyes on her, as well. Later, she enjoyed delivering the mail with Lexington because she could successfully drown out the lunatic's babbling with a custom Pandora playlist on her phone. Lastly, Marc, the old-timer had finished the buildings she was scheduled to do and told her to have a nice lunch.

Like Ice Cube would say, *Today Was A Good Day!*

The homely Polish restaurant begins to pick up a little crowd as she pays the cashier for her order. She glances out of the frosted window and observes Divine parking her loaded mailcart under a tree before rushing inside of the restaurant. The petite carrier removes her postal parka and then plops in the front booth over by the window.

The chubby cook behind the counter yells out, "...*your food is ready!*" to Divine. She nods and at that moment notices Cadina. The petite carrier flashes a weary smile and motions her over. Cadina grabs her new hat and makes her way to Divine's table.

"You know, for a while, I was the lowest employee on the totem pole at Midway, so you know *I'm* glad to see you!" Divine sticks out her hand. "I'm Divine."

"Cadina." She shakes the tiny hand while taking a seat across from her.

The waiter arrives with the food.

"Appreciate you," Divine says to the waiter. She then smiles at Cadina. "Girl, all I had was a banana this morning, so I'm about to put a hurtin' on this right here, you hear me?"

"Go right ahead!"

Cadina laughs as her new coworker begins buttering her pancakes. A beautiful young lady with a stubby little nose, feline eyes, and a smile which illuminates her almond-colored complexion like a burning candle on a cozy Christmas Eve.

"So, you haven't been a carrier that long?"

Divine takes a sip of orange juice before answering. "Just a little over a year. My brother, Freeman, told me the post office was hiring, so I took the test and here I am."

"Freeman..." Cadina repeats. "Isn't he supposed to train me on the truck?"

Divine frowns. "He was, but I don't think he'll be training anybody anytime soon. He was involved in an accident this morning."

"Oh, my God..." Cadina's mouth hangs open. "Is he okay?"

"Other than his pride, he's alright. No one was hurt."

"See, that's why I'm hesitant about driving any kind of truck," Cadina confesses. "I know *I'll* be a nervous wreck...and dealing with the psychopath drivers out there, too-"

"Tell me about it. We lost our mother to a hit and run just three months ago."

"Nooo!" Cadina cups her mouth. "I'm *so* sorry-"

"Thanks. It's been rough, Lord *knows* it's been rough." Divine slows down eating while reflecting. "But I'm dealing with it the best way I can, you know? But as for Freeman? He has his own way of mourning, which is why he's in the predicament he's in now."

Cadina nods in sympathy.

"I see you're making a lot of friends already."

"Lexington is going to be a handful; I see that already," Cadina admits. "But everyone else has been really cool."

"Including Velour?"

"Especially her. She really embraced me with opened arms, schooling me on the do's and don'ts in the postal world-"

"That's cool and all but let me school *you* on a little something." Divine leans in closer to Cadina, staring dead into her eyes. "Everything that glitters, ain't gold, especially when it comes to the likes of her. Not hatin' or throwing any shade, just watch the company you keep, that's all I'm saying."

By the tone of the petite carrier's voice, Cadina has the feeling Divine is not particularly fond of the station's diva.

She decides to change subjects.

"Well, I'm done for the day, but it looks like you can use a helping hand."

Divine shakes her head. "I'm good. I only have two bags left. Enjoy the moment, it'll be over soon enough and that's when the fun really begins."

"I guess I have a lot to look forward to." Cadina rises. "I'll see you tomorrow."

"It was nice meeting you, Cadina."

"Likewise."

Cadina pulls her new cap-flaps over her ears, slips on her gloves, and heads outside to face the bone-chilling temperature. She retrieves the empty mailcart from the side of the building and then sneaks one more peek through the restaurant's window at Divine.

The petite carrier opens a small bible to read while gobbling down her pancakes.

So, Divine despises Velour for some unknown reason.

The stiff winds release an unwelcoming swirl around Cadina, blowing newspapers and other sidewalk debris at her boots, prompting a fast-paced journey back to the station.

FREEMAN

*F*reeman waits at the door of James' apartment for someone to answer. The door whips open and James, still dressed in his postal uniform, with the phone stuck to his ear, motions him in. Freeman pulls off his snorkel, hangs it on the opposite side of the front door, and walks past the dining room area, which is crammed with large cardboard boxes, clear plastic containers, and overly packed garment bags. He notices furniture disassembled and placed next to the wall. But they still have decades worth of items to break down before the big move date. The purchase of their new house was long overdue.

Entering the living room to join James and Freeman, wearing a blue Patrick Ewing jersey and a melancholy expression, is James' daughter, Janae. "Hey, Uncle Free."

Freeman extends his arms wide. "How's my favorite girl?"

"Meh."

"Everything alright?"

She shrugs. "I've seen better days."

Freeman hugs the skinny nine-year-old tomboy, and the stench of secondhand smoke rushes up his nostrils, catching him off-guard. She hands him a game controller, turns on the Xbox One, and challenges him in NBA Live 14. As Janae methodically dominates the match, Freeman tunes his ears to a scathing, one-sided phone conversation James is having while pacing the floor.

"No, you tell me why my daughter was in some hookah lounge when she was supposed to be with you?" James yells into the phone. "You damn right I'm making a big deal about it! My baby coming home smelling like smoke is a big deal! She was in good hands? The hell you mean she was in—? You know what? She's not going over there anymore. Because you're still not showing me you know how to handle responsibility and she's *your* child! Oh, really, word? I'd like to see that happen! You know what? I can't even talk to you anymore. That's right, I have better conversations with a freaking cat!"

James flings the phone on the sofa and tosses himself right next to it.

Freeman had the unfortunate role of sitting courtside to watch the relationship between James and Janae's mother, LaToya Feldman, deteriorate to the point of no return. Since the day Janae was born, LaToya has proven to be anything but a good parent. Focusing initially on jumpstarting a floundering model/actress/singing career, she eventually decided to pursue the sought-after role of 'video girl'. Landing an appearance in only three videos was enough for LaToya to totally neglect her motherly responsibilities and chase every casting call available with hopes of becoming the next Melyssa Ford or La-La Anthony. The chance of that happening being slim to none, due in part to LaToya's conceited attitude, those embarrassing "casting-couch" rumors, and from what James has confided to Freeman in secrecy, her experimenting with drugs. James has given LaToya enough chances with their daughter, and Freeman feels his homeboy is about to drop the sole-custody bomb on her any day now.

"Yessss!" shouts Janae, with her arms raised in the air. "Victory is mine!"

Walking into the living room wearing blue nursing scrubs and a worn expression on her chubby face is James' mother, Grace. With her stubby hands on her thick hips, the short, brown-skinned woman turns to her grandchild. "Okay, young lady, get out of them stinking clothes and hop in that shower."

"Can I play one more game with Uncle Free, pleeeeze?"

"That will have to wait; you got school tomorrow. Let's go."

"I won't hold back next time," Freeman warns.

"We'll see." Janae hugs Freeman. "Love you."

Grace watches her granddaughter pout her way to the bathroom before turning to James. "What was LaToya's excuse this time?"

"She had the nerve to tell me she had a five o'clock hair appointment for an upcoming video shoot, and she didn't want to bring Nae with her because she would get bored, so she left our daughter with one of the bottom-feeding lowlifes she hangs out with at some hookah lounge. Then she tells *me* that I'm being too overprotective, and I need to stop acting like somebody's grandpa! I tell you this; the next time LaToya sees her daughter; it will be in court. I'm sick of her mess..."

James pushes himself from the couch and storms into the kitchen.

Grace shakes her head as she looks at Freeman. "If it's not one thing, it's another with that child's mother." She then heads to the bathroom to check on her grandchild.

In the late eighties, Brooklyn's Raphael Cordero Junior High School I.S. 302 had been the launching pad for James and Freeman's solid relationship. Even in those scholastic years, Freeman saw in James, the same old-school values that he possesses. Freeman also saw his homey follow his father's footsteps and join the Army, even though the Vietnam vet's life was cut short when James was only one. This left Grace to raise him by herself. After three years in the military, James confessed to Freeman that he was not as gung-ho about the service as he thought he would be. Years later, after working a range of jobs, James accepted a position as a temporary postal clerk. During that period, he had a brief fling with a once shy, but incredibly pretty, LaToya. Soon after their love affair dwindled, LaToya announced she was pregnant with Janae. Now nine years later, James realizes that his baby girl is the only blessing that came out of their acrimonious relationship.

James returns to the room with two long-neck Coronas and hands one to Freeman.

"She left my baby in a damn *hookah lounge*," James repeats to Freeman in disgust. "For a video shoot? Just last month, she left Nae with her cousin and told her that she was going to get a pedicure that wouldn't take long. Six hours later, her cousin found out that she had gone to the club! What the hell is wrong with her, Free? She hollers that she doesn't spend enough time with her own daughter, but then she pulls stupid shit like this."

Popping the top off the beer, Freeman asks, "Are you sure taking it to court is the best thing to do? Mess around, LaToya might throw a brick and shatter your whole game plan, and you wind up losing the joint custody you share now—"

"Nah, bruh. Me and Moms have been documenting her negligence for the past two years. And what the hell am I doing—"

James snatches the Corona from Freeman's hand before he can take his first sip.

"What's up with you?" Freeman shrieks, grabbing for the beer.

"You're on punishment—that's what's up. You forgot about what happened this morning?"

Freeman leans back in his chair. "How many times do I have to tell you the man drove his car into *my* truck—"

"It's not just about that, Free. I really hate to pull your coattail, but you've been trippin' ever since your mom's passing. Supervisors questioning me about your behavior, what am I supposed to say to them?"

"You don't say anything; simple as that. Now, can a brother get some water? Or do I need permission for that, too?"

James side-eyes Freeman before heading back to the kitchen. When he returns, he throws an icy bottle of Aquafina on Freeman's lap. "Tucker wants to see you first thing in the morning. Now, I don't know what that sounds like to you, but it definitely sounds like you need to get your shit together and fast."

"I know." Freeman cracks open the water. "And that's why you're going to give me the best shape up you ever cut in your life."

Grace returns to the living room and sits next to James. "And when he's finished with your hair, Freeman, can you drop me off at work, if you have time?"

"I don't know, Ma," James quips. "Another taxi might hit him."

"What's he talking about, Freeman?"

"Oh, nothing. I'll drop you off."

"Thanks. Now, James, last year we had this same conversation about custody, but you reneged, giving LaToya the benefit of the doubt. You sure you want to go through with it this time because once the process begins, there's no turning back."

"I don't know what else to do, Ma. I tried working with LaToya, but she's proven over and over that she's just an unfit parent." James shakes his head. "I have to focus on Janae's well-being from here on out."

"Okay, well, my coworker has a brother who's a family lawyer. I will get his number and we'll start from there."

"Cool."

Grace pushes herself to her feet. "I have to leave in an hour, so get to cuttin'. I'ma check on Nae."

As she leaves, James shuffles to the closet and returns with his barber kit.

"Grab one of those chairs over there," James orders while flapping open his barber cape.

Freeman pulls up a dinette chair and takes a seat. James wraps the cape around Freeman's neck and fastens it.

James grabs a hair pick and goes to work on Freeman's afro. "You know, Tucker sees potential in you, possibly as a future supervisor."

"How do you know that?"

"She told me this, like six months ago."

"What'd she say?"

James brushes his clippers. "Well, she said, 'your friend has leadership qualities.' And I said, 'yeah, he's always telling people where they can go...'"

Freeman laughs. "I guess they all want me to follow in Lexington's footsteps, but they can have that. I'm not letting nobody stress me out."

"Like the way you're stressing out Tucker and Chapman?"

Freeman peeks up at James. "Just cut my hair, alright? Your Moms is waiting on me."

"Look, all I'm saying is Tucker is an assistant manager now; meaning she's going to have less tolerance for people's bullshit with this new position. So, you better start thinking about something else to win her over with besides a simple haircut...you feel me?"

James powers the clippers.

Leaning his head to the side for James, Freeman stares into space, with his mind formulating a game plan to get back on his assistant manager's good side.

"I'll think of something."

―――◎―――

Freeman climbs out of the Fourteenth Street/Union Square subway station and dips into the first deli shop he sees. He tells the cashier he wants a toasted sesame seed bagel with cream cheese. He grabs a pint of Tropicana orange juice from the cooler and places it on the counter. While waiting for his order, he grabs a batch of red roses from the front of the store window.

Near the magazine rack is a full-length mirror.

He quickly checks his appearance.

Crisp, dry-cleaned uniform underneath his postal bomber. Boots polished to a mirror shine. He turns his head from side to side, admiring the professional tapered job James did to his hair and goatee. Pleased with the overall results, he pays for his items and exits the store.

Feeling about as fresh as the cold morning air, Freeman diddy-bops down Fourth Avenue, full of purpose and vitality. When he turns down Eleventh Street, he spots Shabbazz, who is showing Cadina the morning collection board in front of the station's bay area.

Freeman sizes up the physical beauty of the ponytailed sub in her bright yellow hoodie, blue jeans, black leather coat, and matching black boots.

Man, she fine...

Shabbazz mocks a surprised look and gives Freeman a hearty, half-hug pound. "Please tell me the old Freeman is back and not the one that is causing accidents!"

"Be nice," Freeman smiles. "I'm back and in a better place."

"I heard that. Have you two met?"

"Not properly, no." Freeman sticks his hand out towards Cadina. "I'm Freeman, the one who was *supposed* to train you on the truck yesterday. And you are?"

She shakes his hand. "Cadina Wilson. Nice to meet you—finally, I guess."

They all laugh.

"I know," Freeman says. "And I want to apologize for my actions and my appearance yesterday, that's not how I roll at all."

Cadina reaches for the flowers in his hand. "Awww...now, you didn't have to buy me flowers! I mean, I totally understand—"

"Oh, these aren't for you." Freeman jerks his arm back.

"Oh." Cadina turns beet-red.

"AH-HAAA, HAAAAAA!" Shabbazz doubles over in laughter, with dreads flying everywhere. "Yo, that was cold, Free."

Freeman pulls out a single rose and hands it to Cadina.

"Awww, thank you." Cadina blushes, smelling the rose. She turns to Shabbazz and mocks him. "A-HAAA, HAAA!"

"I see she's fitting in already," Freeman says to Shabbazz.

"Without a doubt." Shabbazz hands Cadina the truck keys. "She'd better not hit anybody out on the street, that's all I'm saying. We'll see you at Wang's for lunch."

"Cool."

"Ready, Cadina?"

"Ready as I'll ever be."

She hands Shabbazz the rose and then pulls herself up behind the steering wheel. She cranks the engine, shifts the gear into drive, and jerks the heavy vehicle out of the bay. *"WHOA!"* is all Freeman hears from Shabbazz, who holds onto dear life as Cadina stutter-drives the truck down the street.

Freeman heads into the station and makes his way toward the manager's office. Suddenly, all the fears he had been subconsciously avoiding, come rushing up to him like an angry linebacker. He calms himself down before knocking on the door.

"COME IN!"

He opens the door and steps inside the office, where the humming of the computer keeps the room from appearing mortuary quiet.

Tucker sits behind the desk with her dark brown eyes fixated on him.

He tries to trade smiles with her but fails miserably as the assistant manager remains stoic, with her fingers planted firmly on the desk.

Clearing his throat, he says, "Good morning, Mrs. Tucker."

"Good morning, Mr. Souls."

He swore he did not see her lips move.

She sits behind the desk with about as much life as a puppet.

Just get it over with, Free.

"I'ma just come on out and say I am truly sorry for the way I spoke to you yesterday and the way I've been acting around here as of late. You know that's not how I operate, and I hope you find it in your heart to forgive me." He hands her the roses and the breakfast bag. "I, uh, took the liberty of buying you breakfast, a toasted bagel with cream cheese and orange juice. And these roses. Tokens of my sincere apology."

She examines the roses. "Thank you, Mr. Souls."

"Hey, no problem at all."

He grabs a seat, feeling relieved.

She places the roses in a nearby empty vase. She then digs into her purse to pull out an envelope and hands it to him.

Flipping the envelope over a couple of times, he peeks at the tight-lipped manager. "What's this, a check or some sort?" he jokes.

She says nothing. Her eyes remain glued on his every move.

He opens the envelope and pulls out the form to read. He then jumps out of his seat as if his pants had caught on fire.

"You can't be serious, Mrs. Tucker! A two-week suspension?"

She rockets out of her chair, displaying every aspect of her authoritative position.

"The suspension is effective today, Mr. Souls, and you will report back to duty the following Monday and not a minute later or you'll be suspended indefinitely."

"This is a joke, right?"

"You see me laughing?"

He plops back in his chair. He cups his mouth to avoid arguing further, as he knows she is just doing her job. He made the bed that he must lie in, so he has no choice but to accept the strict penalty which could have been a whole lot worse.

Still, his stubbornness overrides his common sense.

"Don't you think that's being a little too severe? It's not like the accident was my fault-"

"You're right! It wasn't your fault, Freeman—it was *mine*!" She points down on the desk. "I should've never put you in a situation where you could have harmed someone, including yourself. That was my crucial error. But what I will not tolerate is you challenging my authority like I'm one of your peers, you understand me?"

An uncomfortable silence mounts.

He stares at the wall.

Ashamed.

Tucker returns to her seat. In a calmer tone, she resumes, "Look, we know you and Divine have been going through a rough period with your mother's passing. I've been down that road in my own life, with the passing of my father, so I know the pain. But you're using that pain as a crutch, and it's affecting your job security. You're *way* stronger than that, Freeman. Due to the fact you were raised by a strong, beautiful woman. But is this how you want to represent her legacy?"

He avoids eye contact as tears stream down his cheek.

"I asked you a question, Freeman."

"No, Ma'am."

She hands him a tissue box.

Freeman snatches a couple of tissues and then asks, "So, I start this suspension now or what?"

"Hand me that form."

"Excuse me?"

Tucker hastily motions for the suspension paper. "The form. Hand it to me."

Freeman hands it to her.

Tucker stands to her feet.

"Promise me, Freeman, from this day forward, you're going to revert back to the carrier we hired two years ago; the one that comes to work on time and comes to work *correct*, like you are now." Tucker points the paper at him. "Because I don't like giving these things out. Promise me that."

"You have my word."

She rips the form in half and throws it into the wastebasket. "If that other Freeman ever decides to show his face around here again, the next form will automatically be faxed uptown and that one will be for a month...do I make myself clear?"

"Yes, Ma'am—and thanks."

"One more thing..."

Tucker goes inside the desk and pulls out a business card. She reaches it to him.

"I have a friend who counsels individuals with alcohol use disorders. I encourage you to give him a call."

Freeman shakes his head. "I appreciate your concern, Mrs. Tucker, but I'm not suffering from any kind of disorder-"

"Freeman, from my twenties, well into my thirties, I was in denial about a serious nicotine addiction. I overcame it, thank God, but not without help. There's no shame in being transparent."

Tucker insists on the card.

He reluctantly takes it.

She quickly opens the small bag, pulls out the bagel, spreads the aluminum foil, and then takes a hefty bite. "Thank you for the food, I was *starving*." She takes a huge gulp of her orange juice before returning to her seat behind the computer.

"Should I clock in today?"

"Yes. And I believe Chapman has you assigned to Velour's route. Dante took the rest of the week off to prepare for the parcel post position. Oh, and Freeman..."

"Yes?"

"This conversation stays between you and me. Davenport doesn't know about your condition yesterday and I prefer it stays that way, understood?"

"Uh, yeah."

"Good. Now close the door behind you when you leave."

She explains all of this while focusing on the computer.

Freeman throws his backpack over his shoulder and walks out of the office. As he closes the door behind him, he pauses for a moment and stares at the business card she gave him. He crumbles the card in his hand and tosses it into a nearby trash can.

Exhaling relief, he begins his stroll upstairs to start his new day off on the right foot.

CADINA

From Cadina's perspective, time plays a major factor with Shabbazz. The moment they left the station, the dreadlocked instructor turned his radio to Power 98, slapped his game-face on, and proceeded to train her on all the various driver's assignments without compromising the dizzying pace he had set up for himself for the day.

The morning was somewhat of a blur to her as Shabbazz taught her how to do a mailbox collection run. Shabbazz opted to do the first half of the run so they would not fall too far behind, and that allowed her to get a comfortable feel of the truck while the traffic was still light.

At each mailbox she screeched up to, Cadina watched her instructor dash out of the truck, open and empty out the box, scan it, and close it back up. He would then zoom back into the truck and with wild eyes behind his glasses, point to the next mailbox down the street.

When it was her turn, she felt as if she was on a timer. Every mailbox she opened had an avalanche of mail pouring out of its door. As Cadina bent down to rake the letters inside of the bag, she would cut her eyes at her instructor and muse: *He's got another thing comin' if he thinks I'm gonna rush through this.* When she would fill the bag and drag it back to the truck, Shabbazz would ask, "Did you scan the box?" Rolling her eyes, she would find herself racing back to scan the inside of the mailbox. That question was asked two more times before she finally caught on.

After that assignment was complete, they raced back to the station, handed the collection mail to the mail-handlers, and prepared the truck for the next assignment, which Shabbazz called the early mail-drops. They both loaded buckets of mail into the back of his truck, as well as two hand trucks, before heading down the road for the second time that morning.

If the collection run had not awakened Cadina's dormant muscles earlier, the early-drop assignment all but popped whatever biceps she had in her shocked body. With mail stacked six-buckets high on each of the hand trucks, Shabbazz would lead the way as he swiftly moved his load into numerous buildings on Fifth Avenue and into their huge mailrooms. Cadina, however, struggled to prevent her loaded hand truck from rolling away from her each time.

After that two-hour workout, an exhausted Cadina drives back to the station with Shabbazz, who looks almost as refreshed and relaxed as he did when he clocked in. He cocks his feet up in the passenger seat and scrolls through Facebook along the way.

When they arrive, bundled-up carriers from their section push their carts out onto the sidewalk and stop to yell at Shabbazz, "...*Don't be late with my relays, 'Bazz!*" He smiles and gives them the finger, as he and Cadina rush up the steps to the work floor.

They push skids of heavy relay bags to the elevator lift and down to the loading dock area where they see Roy and Neville, who wave and laugh at them. "*Yo, Cadina, don't let him overwork ya!*" Shabbazz flips them the bird, as well.

After a few back-and-forth trips from the work floor, they finally load the truck to the maximum. This time, Shabbazz sits behind the wheel and pulls off as Cadina peels out of her leather jacket to enjoy a relaxing moment of not doing anything. That moment becomes short-lived as Shabbazz whips around Second Avenue and parks in front of their first relay box. They hop out and open the back of the truck. Shabbazz jumps in the back and hands her about six heavy relay bags to toss into the green box. Trying hard to show her instructor that she is unfazed by the strenuous work, she drags the heavy bags to the relay box and throws them in, one by one. After bouncing from relay box to relay box, stretching from Fourteenth Street to First Street, and then those same streets on First Ave, Cadina is virtually whipped.

She places the last group of bags inside the final relay box, climbs back in the passenger seat, and lets out a deep sigh while wiping the cold sweat from her brow with her forearm. She glances over at Shabbazz, who is trying to conceal his amusement.

"Please tell me you're not laughing at me over there," she says in a tired drawl.

"I'm sorry, Cadina, but the look on your face suggests that you might wanna apply for another less physical job."

And disappoint my father again? Not in your life!

"I'm alright. But please tell me we're through for the day."

"Yeah, that's basically it. We've got the brunt of the work out of the way so now what me and the crew would usually do is either return to the station and wait around for them to hand us more work or go grab something to eat."

She squeezes hand sanitizer in her palm and begins rubbing vigorously. "I have a confession to make."

"What's that?"

"Well, ever since we started this morning, I thought you were rushing because you didn't want to train me, but now I see you don't have time to play around. This ain't no joke!"

"I'm trying to tell ya. It's all about getting off to an early start because, at the end of the day, you wanna get those relays out to the carriers, or they gonna pitch a bitch, trust me. But you did alright for your first day on the truck. I'ma brag about 'cha."

"You think I'll be driving by myself anytime soon?"

Shabbazz nods. "And when you do, just pace yourself. Don't rush for nobody, because you don't wanna have to double back to the station for a missing relay bag or you delivered early drops to the wrong building, especially when the traffic gets crazy."

Cadina leans her head back and sighs. "This is going to be fun."

Shabbazz laughs. "Welcome to the post office! Now let's join the crew for some lunch."

He floors the truck and they roar down First Avenue.

She closes her eyes and enjoys the peaceful ride.

I've seen his face somewhere before.

Sitting inside Wang's Chinese Restaurant, Cadina quietly sips on her wonton soup as the crew—James, Lou, Roy, Neville, Shabbazz, and Divine—partake in noisy conversations over their steaming entrées. She tries not to overtly stare at the wannabe rapper, but he reminds her of somebody from the past. She can't quite put a finger on what period of her life, though. But she won't be asking him anything any time soon as the Latino letter carrier is in a heated exchange with James over his lyrical content.

"But why you gonna call my rhymes garbage?" Lou contests, woofing down his fried rice. "I don't understand that-"

"You *never* understand; that's the problem!" counters James. He turns to Roy. "Why do I keep putting up with him?"

Roy licks his fingers from the ribs' sauce. "I ask myself the same question."

"Because you try to clown me, Roy, that's why I don't ask you anything," Lou retorts. He turns to James. "But I do value *your* opinion-"

"No, you don't," James snaps. "Because if you did, you would've heeded my advice the last two times we spoke, but did you? Nope. If anything, your lyrics got way worse."

"How?"

"*How*? News flash, Lou, we don't call our women, *bitches* like that, we've evolved from that era."

"Man, you know damn well there're bitches all over the world scheming on niggas, and that's a fact, so don't come over here with that, *all women are queens,* shit!"

"He has a point," Neville adds, sipping on sweet tea. "I have a few in my family...just ruthless."

"First of all, Lou, your argument is weak." James drizzles duck sauce over his rice. "All you're doing is falling in line with the rest of the cats who just want to cash in on our culture while compromising our cultural integrity."

"Oh, so now you're calling me a *follower?*"

James turns to Roy. "Yo, what was one of his verses?"

Roy wipes his mouth and comically imitates Lou's rapping style. "*'I'm packin' more meat than Ron Jeremy'.*"

Everyone laughs.

Except for Lou.

"And what about, *'I want those hoes hanging in the rafters.'*? You're married, Lou. You're not embarrassed by any of that?"

Lou shrugs. "Why would I be?"

"Damn!" laughs Neville.

James shakes his head. "Man, if it's like that, you should stick to the party joints you used to write. They're way better than that crap you've been writing lately."

"What y'all fail to realize is, I'm trying to get myself in the industry, by any means necessary." Lou glares at all of them. "Once I'm in, *then* I can flip it to the party joints you like. I'm playing chess, son, not checkers."

"Like I said; you're selling out."

Divine turns to Cadina. "What's your take on it, girl?"

Catching her off-guard, Cadina glances around the table.

All eyes are now on her.

Cadina cuts her eyes at Divine.

Alright, Sister Souljah, don't get stupid now.

Cadina wipes her mouth and says, "The way I see it, Lou, is to stay true to yourself and trust the process because the right audience will eventually find you if you're authentic and you'll wind up enjoying a glorious career. That's my take on it."

"And there you have it," James affirms.

Damn, he's fine! Cadina muses about James while returning to her tea.

Lou eyeballs everyone at the table and waves them off. "Whatever, man. All I know is I'm not trying to solve the world's problems. You think I wanna be a mailman for the rest of my life? I got dreams that are way bigger than this uniform and if that means blending in with the new millennials, so be it. I'ma do *me*, regardless."

"Nobody's shooting down your dreams, Lou—"

"Nah, you said your piece, now let me eat in peace, a'ight?" Lou holds up his hand to silence James and then returns to his food.

"You know he won't talk to us for the next two days," Roy says.

Neville snickers, "Hey, that might be a good thing."

"Here comes your brother, Dee." Shabbazz points toward the front window. "Yo, Free came to work with a pity package for Tucker. Roses, food, looking all sharp; he wasn't playing."

"That's because he knew he'd crossed the line," Divine says.

The entire table turns around to greet Freeman and Velour as they enter the restaurant. They take off their coats and join the packed table.

Roy asks Freeman, "So, how'd it go with Mrs. Tucker?"

"Well, it wasn't pretty, I'll tell you that much." Freeman places his order with the waiter and then directs his eyes around the table. "I was facing a two-week suspension."

"Word?"

"Yep. She let me read the letter first, then she read *me* for about a minute, and finally she tore the letter in half and gave me my last verbal warning. And that was about the gist of it."

"Damn, you are lucky. Had it been Davenport—well, who knows. He likes you, too, Free. You one of them likable muthafuckas, you know that? That's why the crew is always doing shit for your dumb ass."

They all laugh and agree wholeheartedly.

Cadina glances around the table. She can tell these guys have genuine love and respect for one another.

"Yeah, well, it was a humbling experience that I don't ever want to encounter again," Freeman says. "I have to stay focused from here on out and for starters, lunch is on me today for all the times y'all covered for me."

"What about tomorrow's lunch?" Shabbazz asks.

"You better make it a whole week," Neville laughs. "You owe a lot, son!"

Freeman smiles. "Whatever. I got y'all."

"Personally…" Velour injects. "I think the only reason Tucker let you off the hook is that she knew she was in the wrong herself."

Cadina glances at her male coworkers.

They all stopped laughing.

And their eyes are planted on Freeman's little sister.

"Really?" Divine wipes her mouth. "Why would you think that Velour?"

"Well, because she knew about Freeman's supposed condition before he left the building, and her job would have easily been in jeopardy had the wrong people found out about it, so instead of just sweeping the whole incident under the rug, she wants to threaten him with a suspension? I just think it was totally unnecessary."

"Well, I think it was *very* necessary if you ask me," disputes Divine.

"But why? The accident—"

"—My brother needed—"

"—Wasn't his fault to begin with—"

"—Some discipline thrown his way—"

"So, she just wanted to cover up her own misdoing. That's all, Dee—"

"I'm not talking about the accident, Velour!" Divine barks. "I'm referring to everything else prior to that. The excessive drinking, tardiness, or not showing up for work at all. If she had given him that suspension, it would've been justifiable, trust me."

Cadina watches the intense conversation the way she would watch Serena and Venus vie against each other in a title match. But unlike the Williams Sisters, there is no love between these two coworkers, especially on Divine's side of the court.

"But you gotta admit, she's treating your brother like he's never done her any favors in the past."

"*Favors*? What are you talking about?"

"Going to the store to get your boss breakfast or getting her clothes out of the nearby cleaners; these are not listed in the carrier's manual. I'm sorry."

"If that ain't the pot calling the kettle—!" Divine shifts her chair and her whole attitude directly at Velour. "And what about *you*? Every time you see my brother, you ring your little bell, shake your big ass and he goes galloping over to you like a dog in heat! Is *that* in the carrier's manual, Velour?"

Cadina's eyes widen in shock.

The rest of the crew try to conceal their snickers.

Freeman immediately jumps in. "Dee, I think you've said enough, okay?"

Divine turns to her brother. "No! This is between me and your little side-piece, so stay outta this-"

"Look, Dee..." Velour resumes. "I'm not trying to be your enemy here. I'm just as concerned about your brother as everyone else is at this table—"

"Please, he already has a fiancée for that role. He doesn't *need* you-"

"I think you need to shut the hell up before I do it for you," Freeman warns.

Divine eyeballs her brother. "So, you're gonna side with this chick over your own sister? Really?"

"Yes, *really*! Because she's just voicing her opinion like everyone else around this table, but when it comes to *her*, you seem to always have a problem! And who are you to be putting my business out in the open like that?"

"As if that was top secret! *Everybody* knows about your-"

"Everybody knows what, Dee? Huh? And that's another thing with you; you flap your gums a little too much about stuff you don't know and I'm getting sick and tired of that shit! You're not my mother, okay, so stay in your damn place!"

The snickering from around the table ends.

Divine embarrassingly peeks around the table before standing up to grab her coat from the back of her chair.

"Nah, Dee. Sit back down and finish your food," James pleads.

"You heard your friend; I need to stay in my place." Divine digs into her pocket to pull out a ten-dollar bill. She slaps it in the middle of the table. "I have a hair appointment to make, anyway."

Freeman picks up the money and tries to hand it back to her. "I told you, I got the bill—"

"Please...your pockets stay on broke." Divine pushes Freeman's hand aside. "And since I'm getting on your nerves so bad, you can start coming up with your own lies when Lovelle, your *fiancée*, wants to see or hear from you, okay? I'm quite sure you can squeeze her in between some of y'all's conversations."

Divine shoots a dirty look toward Velour before stuffing on her furry postal hat and storming out the front door.

A hush is cast over the lunch table.

"I am so sorry if I said anything out of context," Velour whispers to Freeman. "I mean, I wasn't trying to argue with her or anything."

"You don't have anything to apologize for...that's just Dee."

"I can tell you what's the real problem here," Neville says.

"And what's that?" Shabbazz asks.

Neville points at Lou, who is eating. "If he didn't have them hoes hanging in the rafters, we wouldn't be going through this mess!"

The table erupts in laughter.

"Yo, keep my name out your mouth, a'ight?' Lou cautions.
"Y'all are too crazy around here." Cadina wipes the tears from her eyes.
"You're just now figuring that out?" snickers Neville.
James holds up his glass. "Alright, y'all. Let's switch up the mood with a quick toast."
Drinks are raised, except for Velour's, who stirs a straw around and is still in a funk.
"Let it go." Freeman turns to her. "Dee's skin is thicker than most, trust me, she'll be okay."
Cadina watches Freeman as he caresses Velour's hand.
Okay, Mr. Fiancé.
Velour cracks a smile as she holds up her glass.
James begins his toast. "To our boy, Freeman, for returning back to his former self before he got that ass terminated."
"HERE, HERE!"
"To our new coworker, Cadina, who, on her third day of employment, hasn't thought about quitting just yet."
"HERE, HERE!"
Cadina laughs.
"I got this last part, Jay!" Neville begs.
"Go 'head."
Neville smirks at Lou.
"Say something stupid, Papa-"
Neville stands up. "This is a toast to you, Lou! For showing us that you, too, can have hoes hanging from the rafters and be proud about it!"
"When we get outside, it's gonna be me and you, bitch!"
Instead of getting full from the wonton soup, Cadina was unintentionally fed an abundance of newfound information regarding her coworkers during their round table session–from the questionable lyrical content of the wannabe rapper to the beefy catfight between Divine and Velour, and the obvious "courting" between Velour and Freeman.

As for Cadina, her bright spot was James, who she finds at this very moment, staring into her eyes with about the same amount of passion as she is giving him in return.

And that is a good thing all by itself.

James announces, "If all is said and done, cheers!"

"CHEERS!"

Clink!

FREEMAN

$\mathcal{F}$reeman waits in front of the post office building for James to clock out for the day. As he checks his watch, the employee entrance door swings open. Velour steps out wearing an all-white booty-hugging denim outfit with a white goose jacket draped over it. With a white skullcap pulled over her hairdo and white knee-length Ugg boots completing the wintry look, she resembles a sexy poster-girl advertising for a ski resort.

She saunters right up to his face. "Waiting on James?"

Her words fall on deaf ears.

All he wants to do is throw his tongue down her throat.

"Freeman?"

"Oh, uh, yeah, we're about to secure a U-Haul truck for next weekend."

"I am so happy for him. He deserves it."

"I know. Heading home?"

She glances at her watch. "Yeah, my brother is picking me up. I thought he would've been here by now."

He rubs his chin. "Listen, about my sister's verbal assault on you earlier, she's just-"

"That's water under the bridge," she chuckles. "I, too, have thick skin, so we're good."

"Good, because Dee and Lovelle are extremely close, and…you know how that goes."

"Well, can you blame her for having your best interest at heart?" She grabs his hand. "I mean, c'mon, if I had the privilege of being your woman, I'd love the fact that she would go out her way to defend our relationship. So, I'm okay."

Her underlying message sinks in as they swing their arms in sweet silence. Still, he visions his tongue caressing her caramel-colored lips and struggles mightily to fight back those strong urges.

Out of nowhere, a candy apple-colored Bentley Coupe roars down Fourth Avenue and pulls up in front of them. As the limousine-tinted passenger window rolls down, Raekwon the Chef's classic gem, *Incarcerated Scarfaces*, escapes from the pulsating speakers causing pedestrians to peek in to see if the car belongs to someone famous.

Velour rolls her eyes in obvious admiration. "He just *loves* to make an entrance. Come, let me introduce you to my brother."

He follows her to the luxurious vehicle. She circles around to the driver's side as Freeman bends down to peer through the opened passenger window.

"Give me a minute," she says to her brother. "I need to get a money order."

"You should've done that before I even arrived," he quips.

"I'll make it quick, geez."

"Well, get a move on! Time is money!"

"Freeman, this is my brother, Vincent. Vincent, this is my new route partner, Freeman. You two get acquainted while I run back inside." Velour hustles into the post office's lobby.

"Nice to meet you." Freeman reaches his hand through the window.

Judging by Vincent's iron-clad grip, Freeman assumes he works out a lot. And by the rest of his flossy appearance—a dark-grey wool Kangol cap turned backward, a thick red turtleneck sweater underneath an even thicker butter-soft grey leather jacket, plus a red toothpick roaming in and out of his mouth—Vincent appears to be financially sound.

"Heard a lot about you, Playboy—so what's popping?" Vincent inquires.

"Nothing much. Just trying to keep my head above water."

"Aren't we all."

"I see you're doing quite well for yourself." Freeman's eyes take in the white leather seats with red piping and wood grain interior. "This is sweet."

"Appreciate it. I don't get to play with my toys often, due to my hectic work schedule. So today, I felt like taking this one out and letting it breathe, you know what I'm saying?"

"I can dig it."

"Velour is really excited about you replacing Dante on her route."

"Yeah, I guess she is. But if I had my way, I'd prefer driving over delivering any day-"

"By the way, Playboy; have you seen or heard from that water head fuck lately?"

The question stuns the hell out of Freeman.

He takes a second to size up Vincent's overall demeanor.

Cold, unwelcoming eyes combined with a toothy grin that seems to sneer at him as he waits for a response.

"Excuse me, but who are you referring to?"

"*Dante*," Vincent stresses as if he is offended by having to repeat himself. "Velour told me he'd transferred to another station, but I want to know if his bitch-ass still swings by here from time to time?"

Freeman quickly confirms to himself that he has zero tolerance for this dude's vibe or his line of questioning.

"Is there a particular reason you're asking?"

Vincent belts out a condescending laugh directly at him.

Is this dude mocking me?

The car phone rings.

Vincent stops laughing, pulls the toothpick from his mouth, and points it at him. "Don't worry yourself about it, alright? Just be a better route partner than Dante was. I have to take this call, peace out."

Vincent answers the phone while rolling the passenger window up in Freeman's face.

Velour returns and pauses for a moment to admire her brother's vehicle. "Is this Bentley nice or what?"

Freeman heard her but was still trying to wrap his mind around the Vincent interrogation concerning Dante. "Yeah, uh, real nice."

"Just wait until you see what *I* pull up in at James' housewarming!"

Freeman cocks an eyebrow. "Oh, so now *you're* balling on this level…on a postal check?"

"Hey, I have no kids, I live with my brother practically scot-free, and with all that overtime we're accumulating…the sky has been the limit, you hear me?"

"In other words, you got it like that."

"I believe I do."

Freeman dwells on a certain proposal before mustering up the courage to speak on it. "Check this out; I have a couple of tickets to this play called, *Holler If Ya Hear Me*, that's playing off-Broadway. Are you into plays?"

"What?!?" Her eyes light up. "I've been dying to go, but I could never get my hands on any tickets!"

"Well, would you mind accompanying me to the show?"

Velour blushes. "Wow. I'm flattered, Freeman, but I feel like this is something you should take your fiancée to-"

"Something came up and she won't be able to attend," he lies. "So, I'm just asking a *friend* out for a night on the town–no strings attached."

She grins down Fourth Avenue before turning back to him. "You have yourself a date."

He nods and smiles. "Cool."

"Let's go!" Vincent barks through the window.

She rolls her eyes. "Let me go before I have to hurt somebody."

"I'll call you later."

"I expect you to." She slips into the car and rolls down the window. "And thanks for thinking about me."

"I always do."

She beams.

Taking a deep breath, Freeman searches for enough strength in his heart to at least say goodbye to her brother. "It was a pleasure meeting you, Vin—"

VRRRROOOOMMMMM!!!!!!

The gleaming red Bentley leaves a blood-streaked path down Fourth Avenue, just beating the light.

"I see you met Mr. Personality."

Freeman turns around to James, who is standing a few feet behind him, observing the entire scene. They begin their trek down the block.

Freeman shakes his head. "Dude is a character."

"He's something alright," James shrugs. "He used to drop Velour off and pick her up almost every day, right before you started working here, but then it slowed down to only once in a blue moon."

"It's crazy," Freeman ponders. "She always seems to be curious about my family background, but not once has she talked about hers."

"As if you really care about her upbringing. You ain't slick!"

"Don't start that mess. I hear enough from Dee to last a lifetime."

"Yeah, but you can't deny the fact that she was hitting on the truth a little at the restaurant."

Freeman side-eyes James but says nothing.

"Yo, I don't want to be all up in your business because what you do *is* your business, but are you and Velour—?"

"We haven't done anything, okay?" Freeman bluntly states. "But keep that to yourself; let them other cats keep guessing."

"Gotcha. I mean, because if you two are, then that's your—"

"Damn, Jay!" Freeman stops in his tracks. "If I said we didn't do anything, we didn't do anything-"

"A'ight, chill," laughs James. "Getting all defensive and shit."
"But she keeps knocking on my door, yo."
"Yeah, we can see that."
"And I'ma keep it real with you; sooner or later I'm going to invite her in."
"So, what about Lovelle?"
"What about her?"
"Whoa, it's like that now? I thought y'all were trying to make it work this time."
"Let's not go there, if you don't mind."
"Alright, I'll drop it."

They turn the corner on Twelfth Street and walk across the street.

"Yo, what do you think about our new coworker, Cadina?" Freeman says. "Yo, she is mad *fly*. I had a chance to talk to her this morning and she seems really cool, too…Jay?"

Freeman glances to his side and finds himself walking alone.

He turns around.

James is a few feet behind him halted in one spot, with the goofiest grin Freeman has ever seen in his life.

"The hell is wrong with you?"

"Yo, Free, promise me you won't think I'm talking out my ass, please, hear me out."

"What the—what's up?"

"I think she likes me!"

Freeman bursts out laughing.

"I'm serious, Free…you can stop laughing any time now."

Freeman holds his chest and calms down. "And how do you know this?"

"Yo, ever since we met, she's been staring at a brutha! *Hard!* Even at Wang's when everyone was talking, she kept giving me that look the entire time, I kid you not!"

Freeman waits as James unlocks his doors and they both throw their bags onto the backseat. "Okay, if she's throwing all of this unspoken rhythm at you, then maybe you should step to her."

"I don't know, man. I'm not the smoothest brother in the world. I'll probably get all tongue-tied and say some stupid shit trying to be funny."

"Well, that's on you, Playboy," Freeman jumps into the passenger seat. "She's doing her part by giving you an open invite, now it's up to you to do *your* part. And really, just be yourself, that's half the battle right there."

"I know, I know." James slides in, cranks the engine, and then sits back in his seat, staring out the front windshield. "But she's got those soft, bubblegum lips that always seem to stay wet for no reason...it just makes me wanna grab her by her ears, pull her head towards mine and suck on them bad boys! And she got those curvy hips on that slim frame of hers. Yo, did you peep out her walk? She got that walk—that *strut*, mind you—like she just hopped off a thoroughbred with her bow-legged self...DAMN SHE FINE!"

Freeman chuckles. "If she has you sprung like that, then you need to start making moves, dawg."

"C'mon, man. You know I'm shy."

"Shy my ass! That didn't sound like you were shy a second ago when you wanted to grab her by her ears!"

"Hey, at least I don't have hoes hanging in the rafters like somebody we know."

"And packing more than Ron Jeremy!"

"Hey, that's *way* too much information to be sharing with the bruthas."

"Especially when we know his ass is lying!"

The two childhood friends double over in laughter as James peels off down the street.

CADINA

*B*alsamic glazed steak tips with mushrooms, garlic sauteed spinach, loaded baked potatoes and a fresh tossed salad with walnut dressing is the cuisine for the evening at Cadina's parents' home. She woofs down her plate and guzzles a glass of Ocean Spray cranberry juice in one shot, all the while sharing her journey as a postal employee to her sister, Camille.

"I swear, Cam, I even had help today from my instructor and my back still wanted to lock up on me. I can't imagine me doing that truck run by myself."

So, let me get this straight..." Camille, five years older than Cadina, and beautifully full-figured, sporting a braided swirl hairdo, and a Spelman College sweatshirt, pours herself some juice. "You drive a big postal truck around town and drop off heavy sacks of mail to your coworkers?"

"Yep." Cadina leans back in her chair. "*And* empty out those mailboxes you see on every other corner. That's the first thing on my long list of to-dos every morning."

"You sure you don't want your old job back at the restaurant?"

"Not in this lifetime."

"Well, maybe at another restaurant where you can maximize your culinary skills. What I can't understand is how someone as passionate about cooking as you are, opts to work at a place where you have no desire to be-"

"I never said I had no desire to work at the post office, that's coming out of *your* mouth-"

"You know what I mean. That's why Pops stay on your case so much. You have no sense of purpose, what-so-ever."

"Well, he doesn't have to stay on my case anymore because I have a job to do and I'm going to see it through to the end. Next topic, please."

"Well, at least tell me you have some eye candy to look forward to when you're moving all this mail around."

"There's a few," Cadina's eyes gleam. "They are crazy as hell, though."

Camille jumps to her feet in a dramatic fashion. "See! You said it yourself! The people at the post office are deranged and they're going to drag you all the way *down* to the sunken place! GET OUT! WHILE YOU STILL CAN, GIRL!"

Cadina hollers. "You stupid, you know that?"

"Just looking out for my little sis." Camille throws her coat on and grabs a plastic bag from the counter. "Thanks for dinner!"

"I'll call you later."

Camille leaves out the back door.

Cadina pushes herself out of the seat to take care of the kitchen. As she washes a few dishes, the house phone rings.

She wipes her hands before picking up the handset. "Hello?"

"Hey, Cadina! this is Bianca."

"Heeeeey, Bianca!" Cadina cheerfully greets a childhood friend. "Haven't heard from you in a minute! How's NYU treating you?"

"Girl, I finally completed my master's program in business management, so I'm officially done with school, thank you, Jesus."

"Oh, my God. I didn't know this was your last year?"

"Yep. And I'm so glad it flew by."

"Well, congratulations to you!"

"Thank you! And let me congratulate you on your new job, Miss Mail-Lady! How do you like it?"

"So far, so good." Cadina rubs the lower part of her aching back. "I'm really blessed to have it."

"I know that's right. Listen, the reason I called is that I was kind of hoping you would be interested in catering for my mother's sixtieth birthday which is coming up soon."

Cadina pauses briefly. "You want *me* to cater this event?"

"Girl, yes! I had you in my mind ever since I attended your family reunion last year and was told you were responsible for all the amazing food! I didn't know you could throw down like that! I mean, everything was so delicious and the potato salad? Oh, my God! You just can't eat everybody's potato salad, I'm sorry."

Cadina beams with pride while resuming with the dishes. "Why, thank you!"

"Now, I'd understand if you can't do it, being that you've just started your new job-"

"I would be honored to cater this event for your mother. Just give me the menu, headcount, the date, and I'll fit it in."

"Excellent! Now, let's talk about your fee. We're prepared to offer four thousand for your services. And we'll take care of the food expenses and servers."

Cadina almost drops a plate. "Excuse me, but did you say *four* thousand dollars?"

"The family is willing to negotiate if you decide to counter, but it wouldn't be an issue because I personally want your services-"

"Nooooo, noooo, I'm cool with that, thank you! And I promise I won't let you down, either."

"Girl, you couldn't let us down even if you tried. I'll have the itinerary ready for you by tomorrow. Be blessed and have a good night!"

"You as well!"

Cadina hangs up.

"WOOOOO-HOOOOOOO!"

She does the cabbage patch dance right where she stands.

The momentum of her mood shifts from feeling drained to that of elation as wipes down the kitchen counter. Four thousand dollars, for a day of doing something she absolutely loves. Her heart beats like that of a funky drummer but settles down quickly with fear of what-ifs:

What if I undercook or overcook something? Worse, what if I make something and they think that it's just alright and not worth the money?

But she trashes the negative bashing.

Especially when it comes to her forte.

Not only is she going to wear Bianca's praise as a badge of honor, but she's also going to make damn sure her name is on everybody's tongue before, during, and after that event—

Ohhh, but James' big juicy lips, though...

Cadina struts up the stairs with thoughts of new acquaintances and lucrative beginnings.

JAMES RICHARDS

"*N*o, I said *this* Saturday, not next Saturday…Skillet, listen to me…I know what day I said because *I'm* the one who's moving…so what time are you gonna get to the Bronx? YES, I STILL NEED YOU!...I'm not yelling at you…just be on your way and bring Curtis and Simon with you…yes, I'll pay you when we're done, but meet us in the Bronx, not over here…bye."

Fuck!

James pockets his phone as he trudges out of the tenement building and into the cold Saturday afternoon. He blocks the sun from his eyes while glancing up and down Atlantic Avenue, knowing this will be the last weekend the Richards family will spend in Brooklyn before settling into their new home in the Bronx.

He then stares straight ahead at the U-Haul truck parked in front of the building's entrance. His crew, dressed in either worn sweatsuits or army fatigues, congregate at the rear of the truck.

Tired.

Hungry.

And when he shares his recent news, they are going to be pissed. *Oh, well.*

James slaps on a positive smile and joins his cohorts behind the truck. He peeks inside the packed cargo area if only to properly gather his next words. He then turns around and faces his friends.

All eyes are on him.

Impatient eyes.

He clears his throat while maintaining happy eye contact with the crew. "Well, judging by our current situation, we probably need to make two more trips and we'll be done-"

"BULLSHIT!"

Roy, wiping his steaming forehead, fires off first. "Dude! I told you four hours ago; we're not going to be able to finish moving all of your furniture today!"

"Word. And we started late, too?" Shabbazz adds, kicking a rock down the street. "Yo, why did you pick this size truck, to begin with?"

"I was about to ask the same thing!" echoes Neville, sitting on the truck bumper. "You should've rented a moving company for all the shit you got upstairs."

"Yo, all I know is come eight o'clock, I'm ghost." Lou blows out a cloud of frustration into the frigid air. "You said your uncles and cousins were coming; where your peoples?"

James checks his watch. 5:10 pm. "They're on their way, relax."

"They've been on their way since noon, Jay. Where they coming from, Alaska?"'

Grace arrives from the building with a blissful smile.

"Alright, men," she begins, bubbling with misty-eyed pride. "I just want to say that I really, *really* appreciate you all taking time out of your busy schedules to come help us out. It, it really means so much to us—*oooh!*" She sheds happy tears and then wipes them away. "I'm sorry, it's just that this is the biggest day of our lives and because of friends like YOU!" She points to each crew member. "You all are making our dreams come true by being true servants of the Lord! So, when we get to our new home, I will have the best cheeseburgers and crinkle-cut fries ready for everyone, and for an added treat, Neapolitan ice cream for dessert! You know, the kind with the three flavors; chocolate, vanilla, and strawberry—how does that sound?"

The crew glares at James.

"Sounds good, Ma," he responds, looking the other way.

"Great! Again, thank you. And may God bless each and every one of you." Grace wipes her eyes again before skipping back into the building.

Freeman joins the group with a garment bag over his arm and casually dressed for an evening out on the town.

He turns to James. "Thanks for letting me use the bathroom to freshen up before I leave."

"No problem."

"And where the hell do you think you're going?" Lou asks.

Freeman smiles. "I had a prior engagement that unfortunately fell on today."

Lou turns to James. "Yo, Jay, this ain't right-"

"The man has tickets, Lou. What do you want me to do?"

Lou throws his hands in the air. "This is straight cah-cah, Bro. Eight o'clock, I'm out!"

"You ain't the only one," Roy moans.

Lou, Roy, Neville, and Shabbazz grumble their way towards the front of the truck.

Freeman turns to James. "Hey, if you want me to stay until your cousins arrive, I will-"

"Nah." James sits on the bumper. "This will be the last trip for the day. As you can see, the natives are getting restless."

"Put some food in their bellies, they'd calm down."

"I know, right?" James wipes his brow. "But I am surprised you bought tickets on the same day you knew I was moving."

"I didn't. Lovelle ordered them a while back, but it never occurred to me that it was on the same day-"

"Hold up." James stares confusingly at him. "You said Velour is coming to pick you up, right?"

"Yep."

"So, she's gonna drop you off somewhere to meet up with Lovelle?"

"Actually, I'm taking Velour to the show."

"With the tickets Lovelle bought?"

"With the tickets Lovelle bought for me to use at my discretion."

James shakes his head in amazement. "Wow. Does Lovelle know you're taking someone else?"

"At this point, it doesn't matter."

"But does she *know*–"

"Nope. And I'ma tell you why, since you're so determined to know."

"I'm not picking sides, Free, I just asked a simple question."

"Look, people may have their opinions about Velour and it's cool…that's their right. But for me, she's been a breath of fresh air ever since my mom passed and she's been sincere. Unfortunately, I can't say the same for the person that I'm *supposed* to be engaged to. Hopefully, that answered your question."

James studies Freeman for a moment and decides to let it go. For now.

A taxi rolls up and double-parked behind the truck.

Velour sticks her head out from the backseat window.

"Hey, James! How's the moving coming along?"

"It *was* going good, but you're taking one of my helpers."

"Hey, it was all Freeman's idea. I'm just going along for the ride."

James faces Freeman. "So, I was told."

Freeman hugs James, all the while whispering in his ear. "I can handle my affairs, Jay. Concentrate on moving into your beautiful home."

He winks at James before climbing in the backseat of the taxi.

"I know the housewarming is going to be lit," she says in excitement. "I can't wait!"

"You know how I do. Y'all enjoy."

"We will!"

The taxi pulls off.

Skepticism creeps into James' memory bank.

He recalls not too long ago when Velour barely had two words to say to any of the crewmembers, including Freeman. Basically, she was on some prima donna shit. But no sooner than the passing of

Freeman's mother, she made it her business to be his comforter, knowing full well he was spoken for. Freeman may say Velour's actions are sincere, but he's in a state of denial...because no one else is buying it.

And if Velour's actions are motive-driven...*why?*

They are grown-ass people. No need for me to worry myself about it.

James reaches up and closes the cargo door, locking it shut.

A group of teenage boys burst from the building, tossing a football to one another. One of the boys throws a bullet to James, who catches it and immediately launches a Hail Mary toward another boy who is sprinting down the street. The rest of them follow suit.

Jubilation sweeps over him as he now experiences a severe case of the *no mores*. No more listening to those same teenagers running up and down the hallway like a wild stampede late at night. No more bumping into drug transactions inside the building's stairwell. No more street news of so-and-so got shot by whomever on what floor. No more broken, urine-infested elevators to deal with.

And the list goes on.

We are finally out of this friggin place.

"IT'S GETTING LATE, PAPA!" Lou shouts from inside the truck. "LET'S ROLL!"

James snaps back into the present, circles around the truck, jumps behind the wheel, and pulls off, with Roy trailing them in his SUV.

FREEMAN

"Stop playing..." Freeman says, in awe.
Velour giggles. "I told you."
"You live right *here*?"
"This is where I lay my head every night." She grabs her purse and slides out of the backseat. She turns back to him. "Are you going to walk me to the door?"
Freeman grabs the uber driver's attention. "I'll be back."
Deep in the heart of New Rochelle, New York, he just assumed the uber driver was being a slickster by taking the scenic route to Velour's home as he drove through the ritzy neighborhood known as Bonnie Crest. Somehow, he never envisioned her living in *this* area which is famous for its luxurious English Tudor-style homes.
Sliding out of the vehicle, he never takes his eyes off the two-tone brick, three-storied, castle-like mansion, complete with a three-car garage nestled in the rear.
Velour leads the way through the colossal Victorian iron scroll gate and along the cobblestone walkway to the front entrance. He notices her brother's Bentley parked in front of the garages, along with a Ferrari, A Rolls Royce Phantom, and other luxurious vehicles.
"What did you say your brother does for a living?" he asks.
"He owns a chain of custom car shops."
"Oh, word?"
"Yep, from rims to detailing, to accessorizing rides for several recording artists and actors as well; trust me, he does it all. Been

doing it since the late nineties, and as you can see, it's been paying off quite lovely."

"You got that right."

Before she can stick her key into the lock, the door swings open. A tall, dark-skinned brother, wearing a black mock-neck shirt over his rock-solid frame and matching doo-rag, greets Freeman with a tight-lipped thuggish glare.

"Hey, Stanley." Velour pockets her keys. "Freeman, this is Stanley, better known as Strong. Strong, this is my coworker, Freeman—"

Stanley quickly slams the door before giving her the chance to even finish her sentence.

Freeman gives her a puzzled look.

"A close friend of the family," she explains while shaking her head. "Don't mind him. He just wants to show his ass, that's all."

"Well, the way he was grilling me a second ago, it looked like he could be more than just a close friend."

"*Please.*" She inches closer to his lips. "He's like another overbearing brother I don't need in my life right now."

Freeman momentarily stares at the door before meeting her halfway towards her lips. "Well, what *do* you need in your life right now?"

She grips his face and thrusts her tongue inside his mouth, and they taste each other for the very first time. He matches her intensity to such a degree, they begin play-fighting for tongue domination. They wrap up the passionate moment with laughter and a long, comforting hug.

"You had a good time tonight?" he whispers in her ear.

"The best night I've had in a while."

Between her nibbling his ear and inhaling her enticing perfume, he manages to say, "I'm glad."

She pulls away while still holding onto his hands. "But now I have to get ready for tomorrow. We had a shipment arrive today and we must put the new rims and accessories on display, sooo, that means-"

"Long day tomorrow."

"But don't let it stop you from calling me tomorrow evening."

"And what if I decide not to?"

She purses her lips. "Then, I will pout and call you all kinds of names."

"Oh, really..."

"Yes, really."

They share another long, sensual kiss.

He peeks down at his crotch area. "Okay. Something's popped up. I'll see you Monday."

"Bye, Silly."

After a quick kiss, Freeman double-times it to the waiting uber. "To the Bronx, please. Co-op City."

Freeman turns on his phone.

Thirteen messages.

Eleven from Lovelle. Two from Divine.

Out of nowhere, he hears a loud disturbance.

He turns his head and witnesses Velour having a heated discussion with Vincent that apparently gets out of hand when the muscle-bound sibling repeatedly points his index finger in Velour's face. She, in turn, slaps his hand away from her and stomps her way inside of the mansion. Vincent then turns his attention towards the uber and locks his eyes on Freeman.

What the hell...

After a long and unsettling stare down, Vincent rolls down the sleeves of his black shirt and storms back inside, slamming the door behind him.

"Ooooh, he looked like he wanted to kick your ass, my friend!" the nosy uber driver states. "I hope you have good health insurance—"

"Co-op City, the Bronx, please—thank you."

The uber driver rolls his bloodshot eyes and drives off.

His phone vibrates in his hand.

It's another text from Lovelle.

Instead of responding back to his fiancée, he texts Velour to see if she's alright.

She immediately responds by saying she's good, along with a winky-kiss emoticon.

Lovelle now calls him and he immediately turns the phone off. He does not want to hear her mouth about anything, especially if it pertains to those tickets. If anything, he would love to thank her for purchasing them. But that would be tacky.

Right now, he could care less about his fiancée or Vincent, for that matter. He and Velour had too much of a blast for him to let anything or anyone spoil his erotic high.

Freeman gazes out the window and smiles at the clear blue night.

MICHAEL DAVENPORT

*M*onday morning at Midway Station and Davenport strolls down the work floor toward Chapman's section. With his obligatory 'good mornings' and a politician's 'wave-and-smile', the station manager's professional charade is in full effect.

Behind his pasted grin, however, lies displeasure.

As soon as he gets his station operating at full potential, the powers-to-be from midtown shatter Davenport's stability. This time it happens to be a valuable component of his operation. Supervisor Sterling, his truck/computer specialist, who also possesses the experience needed to manage another station, will be used in that capacity for a three-month period until the folks from midtown can permanently assign someone else.

The aggravated manager takes off his coat and shakes Chapman's hand. "How's it going?"

"It's going. Denise told me the jolly news about Sterl."

"They just can't keep their hands out of my cookie jar," Davenport gripes. "I must be doing something right if they're always willing to pull people from *this* station instead of the other stations in this city."

"I agree with you on that. When's he leaving?"

"In another month. And you'll be taking Sterling's spot downstairs for the duration of his absence."

"Who's going to take my spot up here?"

Davenport crosses his arms. "Take one guess."

"Someone straight from the Supervisor Academy. Can you say *sacrificial lamb*? I feel sorry for the person already."

"I know. How're we looking around here?"

"Marc called earlier this morning, saying he couldn't make it in today."

Davenport lowers his brow. "What's wrong *this* time?"

"He said he has to change medications because the ones he's currently taking are making him sick."

The manager grimaces.

"I specifically asked him to consider either staying home until he was one hundred percent healthy or taking a light-duty position, to avoid putting too much strain on his body, but he wants to play this on and off crap and I'm getting a little tired of it. Who is on his route today?"

"Miss Wilson."

Davenport nods. He makes his way over to the workstation where an overwhelmed Cadina is standing in one spot watching the mail handlers stack up two columns of overly packed letter trays that measure up to her waist.

"Miss Wilson!" he greets in a jolly tone. "How're we making out over here?"

"Okay, I guess."

"From what I'm hearing, you're doing a magnificent job. Keep up the good work, okay?"

"Thank you."

Davenport returns to the podium where Chapman prepares to brief him.

"I spoke to Freeman and Lou about pivoting over to help Cadina when they're done. James is going to swing by Divine's route after she's finished, so everyone's covered."

Davenport nods. "Good. We need to bring everyone back early to the station as soon as possible. The folks at midtown are hounding me about the excessive overtime we accumulated after the holidays and they want things to start smoothing out now. What they need to do is to stop taking my staff away from me so that I can successfully follow through with what they want."

"I'll make a note of it." Chapman scribbles on his clipboard. "I'll keep you posted with everyone's whereabouts."

"Thanks, David. I'll be in my office if you need me."

Davenport makes his way down the work floor, shaking hands, smiling, and waving. Yet, as he hits the stairwell, he thinks about how nice it would be if he could persuade the folks at midtown to leave his staff alone.

CADINA/LEXINGTON

*A*ches and pains travel throughout Cadina's body as she labors up the loading dock ramp and onto the elevator lift. When the doors close, so do her eyelids. She summons enough nerve to pose a daring question to Chapman pertaining to the party she is supposed to cater for the upcoming Saturday. The thought of calling in sick did cross her mind, but she quickly dismisses the notion. After that whole restaurant debacle with her father, she is sticking to the promise of cleaning up her act, which means no more doing what she wants to do when she wants to do it.

But we're talking four grand, Boo.

Her heart flutters with the possibilities.

She quietly recites to herself; "*I would like to have this Saturday… nah, that's too direct…Would it be possible to have this Saturday off for an event I was asked to cater?*"

The elevator reaches the second floor.

The doors open and there stands Lexington, dressed in a two-piece gray wool suit, a greased-down baldie, and an even greasier-looking smirk on his face.

He swaggers onto the elevator with one hand in his pocket and the other holding a cellphone. "Good morning, Cadina. Today's the big day!"

She stares right through him. "Excuse me?"

"The supervisor exam; I mentioned this to you on several occasions. Don't tell me you forgot?"

"I didn't know I was supposed to remember. But good luck, anyway."

She walks off the elevator lift.

"Chapman told me you're going to be on my route today." Lexington presses the button. "Don't make me look bad."

Cadina spins around to the shiny-face rascal. "That was really encouraging, Lex."

"Just messing with you. I'm sure you're going to do what you can."

Lexington smiles down at his phone as the doors close.

Asshole.

She gets her mind right before walking down the work floor, en route to the podium where Chapman is hanging up the phone.

"Good morning, Mr. Chapman," she greets, while also measuring the supervisor's mood. "I was told I will be covering Lexington's route today?"

"Shabbazz won't be coming in, his car broke down on the highway this morning." He explains this while erasing something from his clipboard. "Which means you'll be covering his truck assignment."

Her heart sinks completely through the floor.

"B-But I only trained a few days with him on the truck—"

"We know. This is his collection board." He hands her the folder. "You're only doing that and his relay runs today. Roy is going to drive you to the garage to pick up the truck, so meet him downstairs, he's waiting on you."

This was not the type of morning she was anticipating.

"Wow, okay. Um, but I have a favor to ask from you."

Chapman continues jotting on his clipboard. "What is it?"

"I was wondering if it would be possible to have this Saturday off?"

His eyes pop up at her.

You would have thought she cursed at him.

He shakes his head. "I'm sorry, Miss Wilson, but being that this is your probationary period, I have you locked in on every Saturday for the next three months due to filling in vacation spots, carriers' three-day weekends, plus the fact that we're still undermanned in this station. I'm afraid I can't give you this Saturday off."

Her mind goes to work.

"I understand, Mr. Chapman, I really do, but I'm supposed to cater my aunt's birthday this Saturday and my family is counting on me to do this. I promise I won't bother you about any more days off, I swear."

She hits him with her best puppy dog expression.

At that crucial moment, Tucker joins them at the podium.

"Did you hear from Shabbazz?" the assistant manager asks Chapman.

"Just got off the phone with him. Cadina is going to cover his truck assignment today, but only the collections and relays. Roy and Neville are going to split up the early drops. And I know you heard the news about Marc…"

"Yeah, the doctor prescribed him the wrong medication. I tell ya, if it's not one thing, it's another." Tucker gives Cadina a once-over look. "Good morning, Miss Wilson. Are you ready to go?"

"Yes, Ma'am."

For some reason, Cadina is not feeling any positive vibes from Tucker at all.

But then, the unthinkable is about to happen.

Don't you dare ask her, Chaps, please don't ask her—

"Not to jump subjects, Denise," Chapman says. "…but Miss Wilson wants to know if she can have this Saturday off to cater a family event."

Tucker furiously shakes her head. "Your Saturdays are booked for the next couple of months, my dear. Didn't you see the schedule before you made plans for this event?"

Cadina starts fast-talking.

"I know this is short notice, Mrs. Tucker, but I wouldn't be asking if it wasn't important."

"Well, I'm sorry, Miss. Wilson, but they're going to have to find another caterer for this affair. It's only Tuesday, they'll have enough time."

"But they don't want anybody else, they want *me*."

"They do know you just started a job that requires you to work on the weekends, right?"

"They know this already, Mrs. Tucker, but I—"

"But you went ahead and made a commitment, knowing you were scheduled to work this Saturday?"

Cadina pauses for a second to get her answer straight. "Well, yes, but only because I didn't think it would be too big of a deal to have that day off—"

"Let me explain something to you, Miss Wilson," Tucker tightens her lips. "When we hired you as a part-time flexible substitute, it meant just that. You must be flexible with *our* schedule, not the other way around. You see what's happening around here. Lexington is about to leave soon for the academy. Marc is dealing with health issues and then you run into situations like Shabbazz's. So, if I were you, I would call your people and tell them you can't fulfill that obligation, okay? I'm sorry. I'm so sorry."

The expression on Tucker's face suggests that she is not really sorry at all.

"Now, if you run into any problems during your collection run, don't hesitate to call us or one of the drivers, they would be happy to assist you. And please be safe out there."

Tucker turns around to continue chatting with Chapman.

"AYE, CADINA! LET'S GO!" Roy yells from the elevator lift.

Cadina turns around and marches down the work floor.

Each stride is fueled with anger and resentment.

She could've given me the damn day off. It's not like the whole station is going to suffer because of my absence.

Despite it all, she must push those bitter emotions aside to concentrate on a truck assignment she has no desire of doing.

She quickens her pace to the elevator.

POSTAL REBOOT 139

Inside midtown Manhattan's general post office on 33rd and 8th Avenue, the examination room is crowded with jittery supervisor-hopefuls, who quietly wait for the test administrator to signal the start of the first part of the exam.

An attractive Dominican woman becomes so annoyed with Lexington trying to gain her attention, that she boldly displays her wedding ring. He turns around in his seat and stubbornly adjusts his bowtie.

"Okay, everyone!" the tester says, motioning for the classroom's attention. "You will have thirty minutes to complete the first part of this exam. When I say time's up, you put your pencils down immediately and close your booklets. Any questions?"

Adrenaline rushes through Lexington's body every time he thinks about his future transition from a person delivering mail to a person who *oversees* the people who deliver the mail. His mind travels four to five years down the road where he sees himself navigating in the supervisory field until he has gained the time and knowledge needed to achieve his ultimate goal —becoming a station manager. The endless opportunities cause him to tremble in sensation.

"You may open your booklets and begin."

The flapping sounds of pages turning echo throughout the large room.

Lexington grabs his pencil and focuses on the task at hand.

HOOONNKKK!!!!!

Cadina snaps out of her trance and realizes the light has turned green. Before she can release the brake, the truck behind her blows its horn again.

"OKAY, ASSHOLE!" she screams from inside the truck as she drives down Second Avenue on her way to drop off the last of the relays.

What a day.

Everything that could've gone wrong, did. Not only did the early collection go haywire (letters flying into the streets because of rapid winds, a couple of mailboxes she couldn't locate on the streets only to find out they were inside buildings, and she had to turn right back around to scan a couple of boxes she missed), but with the few early mail drop-offs she had to deliver, she took them to the wrong buildings-

This address is 30 East 9th, my dear, not 30 East 10th.

And that string of unfortunate events made her late getting the relays out to her coworkers. Each carrier she met up with either gave her a compassionate look or was obviously ticked off by receiving their relay bags an hour late. A few carriers were happy with the slow relay delivery, only for the sake of overtime. But she wasn't happy at all. Only tired.

Pulling up to the final relay stop for the day, Cadina watches an older female carrier near the relay box swing her arm impatiently as she talks on her cell phone.

Cadina can only assume that the conversation is about her.

She parks the truck, stumbles out of the passenger's side to open the back door. The woman carrier hastily motions for Cadina to bring the bags over to her opened mailcart.

The woman carrier snaps in the phone, "Noooo, she's here now, so what do you want me to do? An hour is definitely not cutting it." She swings around to Cadina. "Are these your last relays?"

Exhausted, Cadina nods yes.

"Yeah, I'm her last stop…Yeah, I'll tell her, bye."

The woman carrier pockets her phone and releases a disappointed sigh while shaking her head at Cadina. "Chapman wants you to help me finish up my route so I can get back within the hour, as if that's going to happen. Did you eat yet?"

"I'm alright."

"What does that mean?" the woman carrier huffs. "Yes or no? You're entitled to your lunch, you know?"

"I said I'm alright."

"Okay."

The two ladies load up the cart with four relay bags.

"Your name is Cadina, right?" the woman carrier asks, pushing up her glasses on her nose and sticking out her hand. "My name is Gladys. I just don't want you dying out here on me, alright?"

"I understand."

"Well, you ready?"

"Let me lock the truck."

Cadina just lied to the lady. Her stomach is grumbling up a storm.

But she prefers to wait until she's at home to eat. That way, she can soak in a hot bubble bath afterward and then jump into her cozy bed which is calling her with each passing minute.

Cadina wipes her face with a small towel, grabs her jacket, and then locks the truck. She turns around and watches Gretel push her cart down the sidewalk, which is fine by her. At this very moment, she is not in the right frame of mind to get acquainted with another one of the elder carriers.

Tucker killed that mood earlier that morning.

She purposely trails behind Gretel with hopes of a better tomorrow.

The next day does not do Cadina any justice at all.

In fact, it starts off on the wrong foot in a hurry, as the relaxing bath she took the night before evidently overdid its job. She wakes up late, hurries a shower, throws on some clean work clothes, and bolts out the door without even applying make-up.

As Lexington sits on his bed to tie his shoes, the radiance of the sun blasting its way into his bedroom, causes him to chuckle with delight. His future appears just as bright.

He knows he aced that test.

He can just *feel* it.

Now, all he has left to do is to impress the members of the board, which to him, is merely a welcome wagon for the future elite, and his mission will be completed. He laughs as he checks his neat appearance, grabs his leather trench, and struts out the door.

"*Dumb-asses...*" mutters Cadina as she washes her hands and arms.

Another day. Another truck assignment. Another dramatic episode. It was bad enough that every collection box on Neville's run was stuffed with oversized mail, but she failed to see the humor in finding a mushy Big Mac sandwich inside the last box. This caused her to squeeze secret sauce over some of the mail and her arm. After cleaning herself off, she hurries downstairs to load up the truck with the early drops. Repeating to herself simply to take it easy, she does exactly the opposite. She rushes through her early stops only to find out that some of the mail was delivered to the wrong buildings—again.

These people are going to think I'm stupid.

More time wasted. Extra energy spent. After correcting those errors, she high tails it back to an empty station. Panic overtakes her body as she pushes heavy relay skids to the elevator. She does not want a repeat performance of yesterday's disaster. When she arrives at the loading dock, she launches the heavy bags into the truck, slides behind the wheel, and takes off down the street.

Just like the previous day, carriers wait by their relay boxes for her arrival. She apologizes to each carrier for being late and again she receives mixed reactions. This time, however, it doesn't faze her as she delivers the last of her relays. She parks the truck on a side street, turns off the engine, and closes her eyes.

Whew.

Finally, she gets to rest.

With her heartbeat settling down to its regular pace, she cannot recall ever working this hard in her life. She never had to. Everything was inadvertently handed to her on a silver platter. Slowly those pampered walls are being broken down by the physical realization of her current job.

Cracking her eyes open slightly, her attention is drawn to her feet. She reaches for an item tucked behind her route board.

She stares at it in horror.

An Express envelope needed to have been delivered by noon. And it's now three in the afternoon.

She cranks the truck, slaps the gear into drive, mashes the gas pedal, and roars down the street, desperately repeating, *"oh my God, oh my God!"*, to herself. As she drives the late item to its destination, she is cut short by a construction flagger, who furiously waves his stop sign as if he is about to hit the front of the truck.

She looks left.

A funeral convoy, stretching a mile long, creeps through the busy intersection.

You're in big trouble, Caddy.

She shifts the gear in park and slouches back in her seat to watch the limousine-led vehicles, shining their bright lights, pass by.

In Cadina's eyes, failing to deliver the Express envelope, which she now held in her trembling hand, was like watching her own funeral take place.

Lexington is loving every minute of it.

He now stands proudly before three board members.

Armed and ready to show them he possesses the proper skills needed to lead the masses.

From the first question, *"Why do you want to become a supervisor?"*, to the last, *"What is the number one goal of a supervisor?"*, Lexington confidently answers with integrity and professionalism. He wishes Davenport was present to witness his student emulate his style. He would be proud.

The board members rise to their feet to shake his hand and commend him on a job well done. He holds back his emotions until he leaves the room.

Mission complete.

In the hallway, he feels like he's floating in air. He tries to hold back his solo celebration but cannot contain himself.

"YEEEEEEEEEEEAAAAAAAHHHHHH!"

His reaction scares a lady custodian half to death.

"Sorry!"

He laughs out loud, as he runs down the corridor, pumping his fist in the air in victory.

CADINA

*C*adina sanitizes her hands and digs into the corners of her eyes to make sure there is no crust buried in them. Then she applies her lipstick. Afterward, she checks her face one last time in her compact mirror and then hops out of the truck. She locks the door, and turns around to take a deep breath, for this will be the first time that she has ever worked with James alone and she plans on keeping her emotions under control.

She pushes through the revolving doors of an impressive co-op building and is quickly greeted by a pot-bellied, black uniform-wearing Spanish doorman, who is handling luggage.

"May I help you, Ma'am?" he asks, under his thick mustache.

She flashes her postal badge.

He smiles. "James is in the back." He points her in the direction of the mailroom.

"Thank you."

Cadina walks to the back room. She observes James as he places bundles of mail in their designated panels.

With his headphones on, he bobs his head to his music before doing a quick double-take at Cadina. His surprised gaze turns into a welcoming grin as he pulls off his headset.

Her heart flutters in delight.

"I thought you'd be on your way home by now," he says.

Hmmm. He's been thinking about me.

"I thought so, too." She leans on the ledge. "But Chapman wanted me to check on you to make sure you were alright out here."

"All I have left is this building, so if you want to give me a hand, you can start on the other end."

"Sure, no problem."

She heads to the panel but turns around immediately. "Uh, James, question; would I be in trouble because of this?" She pulls out the Express receipt from her jacket and shows it to him. "It didn't get there before twelve."

James examines the receipt. "Nah, it was attempted yesterday."

"What does that mean?"

"It means that somebody tried to deliver it yesterday, but no one was home, which means the next day you don't have to rush trying to deliver it before noon. So, you're good."

"Thank God."

"You were shook for a minute, huh?"

"Man, you don't know the half!"

Their hearty laughter slows to a light chuckle. The attraction she feels for him is too overpowering to conceal. She sees it in his eyes as well. They quickly head to opposite panels and begin working.

For the next ten minutes, the only sound in the mailroom is the opening and closing of the panel doors. They talk for a brief spell about the job, but then silence again fills the room.

She analyzes the challenge that lies ahead and takes it upon herself to jumpstart their flat-lined conversation.

She did not dig the crust out of her eyes for nothing.

She picks up a letter that does not have an apartment number on it and strolls over to him.

"Uh, 16B."

"Thanks." She returns to her panel and then turns around. "What's the name of that cologne you're wearing?"

Beaming with pride, James replies, "It's called Iceberg Twice. Why? You like it?"

"Well, you sure sprayed a lot on."

She resumes delivering the mail.

From the corner of her eye, she is pleased to see the results of her smart remark.

Laughter.

Yes!

He turns to her. "Now, I know you're not cracking on my cologne over there."

She turns around and smiles. "I'm saying, though. Just a little dab will do you, James, not half the bottle, c'mon."

"I see you come with jokes. Okay, you got that one."

"I'm only messing with you. It smells nice."

"I know damn well it smells nice! And for your information, I didn't spray half a bottle on me, either."

"Then how much did you put on, a quarter of a bottle?"

"Let's just say I sprayed enough to grab *your* attention."

He's flirting...about time!

She grins. "I'm scared of *you*."

"You don't have to be."

The tingling sensation hits the Richter scale in her body.

"Alright, now."

Earth, Wind & Fire's classic song, *Devotion*, softly harmonizes from the lobby/mailroom speakers.

"Ahhh, yeah." Cadina sways her head and snaps her fingers. "This is my jam right here!"

"What do you know about Earth, Wind, and Fire? That's *my* group–"

"Mine, too! That's all my father played growing up! Them and the Isley Brothers."

"So, you got it honestly, huh?" James croons in a high falsetto, "*Through Devotion...*"

"*Blessed are the children!*" Cadina joins in, with her arms stretched out in dramatic fashion.

They sing so hard that they catch the eye of a tenant who walks in on their serenading act. The tenant retrieves her mail from the box, smiles at both James and Cadina, and then exits the mailroom.

"You crazy, you know that, right?" he says.

"Well, you started it!"

"Can I get your opinion on something?" He digs in his hoodie pocket.

"Sure. What's up?"

She strolls over to him and for a moment, gets lost in the scent of his cologne, which she is already growing to love. He opens a flyer and points to two pictures.

"I'm having somewhat of a dilemma here. I want to surprise my daughter with a bedroom theme for the new house. Now, she loves Beyonce, but she's also a devoted Knick fan. I can't decide between the two."

She smiles half-heartedly at the flyer.

"Well, I mean, does my opinion really matter? What does her mother think?"

"Her mother isn't around anymore."

Her mouth gapes out of sheer stupidity for sounding jealous. "I'm so sorry, James. I didn't know she had passed—"

"No, no, no..." He waves off her assumption. "Let me rephrase that. When I say she's not around, I mean she's...she's just not active in her daughter's life. As crazy as it sounds, that's the reality I'm dealing with, so..." He stuffs the flyer back into his pocket and resumes to his panel.

"Oh."

Too judgmental, too soon.

Clean it up, Cadina, switch topics.

"So, do you have a picture of your little angel?"

James turns around. He grins like a proud father. "I sure do."

He pulls out his wallet, fingers through his credit cards, and business cards, to no avail. He gives her a sheepish look and flips through his wallet again. "It's in here somewhere."

She folds her arms. "Now that's a shame."

"I just bought this wallet two days ago and I thought I transferred everything from my old one—"

"You know, there should be a *law* against this type of foolishness."

"You know what?" James pockets his wallet. "Just for that remark, you're coming to my housewarming party this Saturday so you can meet her yourself, and I'm not taking no for an answer, either."

She laughs but then studies his face. "You sure it's cool?"

"What did I just say?"

His sense of humor matches hers to the tee. Even though she knows to take this one day at a time, she has a good feeling she is going to enjoy the beginnings of this newfound friendship, and whatever else it may lead to. She just hopes he is on the up and up about this "supposed" baby-momma drama. Nothing in life is what it seems these days. She knows this for a fact. But her inner voice has already confided in her.

He is the chosen one.

"Okay, but I'm not coming over empty-handed, so can I bring over a dish?"

"You cook?"

"I dabble a little."

"A little..."

"Well, a lot. I enjoy cooking."

"Well, surprise me with your culinary skills."

"I will do that."

"Cool."

All the qualities of what a man should be are being portrayed right in front of her eyes. Confident, but low-key. Gentle when he needs to be. Strong when he has to be. And the ability to laugh at himself and not take life so seriously. She is digging him more and more with every passing second.

"James..."

He stops working and turns her way.

"Go with the Beyonce theme. She's doing a lot better than the Knicks these days."
James' face lights up from laughter.
They continue to work and converse in pure harmony.
Like life-long companions.

LEXINGTON

*O*utside of Midway Station, Lexington leans on the building as he impatiently waits for Tucker to stop chatting with James' mother, Grace, and daughter, Janae. He checks his watch. She said to give her five minutes. Yet, fifteen minutes have blown by, and the two ladies haven't stopped to catch their breaths.

The rumbling sounds of a truck bend Lexington's ear.

He turns around and watches Cadina park the postal truck on the curb and hop out on the driver's side. He smiles but then frowns once he sees James jump out of the passenger's side. The two carriers walk in his direction, laughing and smiling at one another.

He immediately waves at her. "Hey! How was your day-?"

They stroll past Lexington and join the gathering on the corner.

Lexington grimaces as he checks his watch again and stubbornly listens in on their extended conversation.

James embraces both his mother and daughter. "Cadina, these are my two sweethearts. My queen, Grace, and our future WNBA first-round draft pick, Janae."

"Nice to meet you," Grace said, vigorously shaking Cadina's hand.

"Nice to meet you, too, Ma'am." Cadina turns to Janae. "Hey, Pretty."

"Hey."

The pigtailed young lady, in her pink goose jacket and matching Nikes, slowly encircles Cadina, inspecting her body.

Confused, Cadina looks over her shoulder. "Is something on my back, Sweetie?"

Janae turns to her father. "Daddy, why did you tell Uncle Freeman she has an onion booty? Clearly, her booty doesn't look like no onion."

James turns red from embarrassment.

Cadina blushes.

Lexington fumes by the wall.

Cock-blockin' bastard!

"I don't know what she's talking about," James responds, chuckling. "But I, uh, invited Cadina to our housewarming Saturday, Ma."

"Oh, she's already welcomed." Grace smiles at Cadina. "And I'm happy Denise is coming, as well!"

"Wouldn't miss it for the world." Tucker hugs both Grace and Janae. "Now, if you'll excuse me, I have to finish up for the day. It's always good seeing you, Grace."

"Likewise."

About time.

Tucker walks over to him with a grand smile. "Sooo, Mr. VanGuard, are you ready to spring the good news on Davenport?"

Despite being annoyed by James and his family's presence, Lexington cannot stifle his giddiness any longer. "Let's do this."

They make their way inside the station.

Lexington overhears Cadina relieving herself from James and his family.

He approves of a thought that enters his mind.

"On second thought, why don't you go and break the news for me while I use the bathroom."

Tucker gives him a curious look. "I can wait. I'm quite sure he'd want to hear the big announcement from you."

He hears Cadina walking up the ramp. "I'm cool with you doing it. It's no big deal, either way."

"Well, if you insist. Shoot, I think I'm more excited than you are at this point! Meet me in the office." Tucker winks at him and then double-times down the first floor.

With his heart racing, Lexington waits to hear the door behind him open so it won't appear as if he was waiting for her. The next five seconds seem like an eternity to him. Finally, the door swings open and Cadina enters the building's stairwell.

He turns around and mocks a surprised expression. "Oh, hey Cadina!"

"Hey."

She passes by him and approaches the area called the valuable's cage to return her arrow key and registered mail receipts to the clerk.

Lexington obsessively appraises Cadina's toned profile.

Her long, black ponytail that rests on the back of a track athlete's frame.

Her cute bow-legged stance.

Her firm onion booty.

He has been craving her body from the moment he first laid eyes on her. But due to his tight schedule and her training sessions on various truck assignments, he has never had the chance to establish any kind of connection with her. Therefore, he must act now.

She tells the lady clerk *thank you* and heads back to the stairwell. And just when she's about to take the staircase, he cuts her off.

"Guess what?"

Annoyed, she asks, "What?"

"I got a ninety-eight on the exam!"

"You got a ninety-eight on what ex…ohhh! The supervisor's exam! Congratulations! That *is* good news! I'm so happy for you!"

"Really?" The excitement in her voice makes his private jump. "Thanks! That test would've been a beast had I not prepared for it with Davenport's help."

"Good for you, Lex. That is really major! Congratulations again."

She tries to go around him, but again, he blocks her path.

"Lexington, what do you want from me?"

"Well, I was wondering if you wouldn't mind accompanying me to a celebration dinner later this evening—"

His proposal is met with a declining headshake.

"I'm sorry, Lex, but I have a ton of stuff to do when I get home, so–"

"I know this was short notice, but what about tomorrow? I'm free as a bird!"

"Lexington...can I be honest with you?"

"Noooo, I'd rather you take me up on my offer."

"But I'm not interested in you in that way."

"Oh, really?" His tone stiffens. "You haven't been around me long enough to form a true opinion about me."

"Hold up, Lex. How are you going to tell me about my own feelings towards you?"

"Because you don't know any better, that's why."

"Excuse you?"

The intense exchange is cut short when James enters the stairwell.

"Hey," James says to Cadina while squeezing in between the two of them. "I told my moms you're bringing a dish to the party and she wants to know what it is."

Cadina rubs her chin. "I was thinking about making oxtails–"

"*STOPPP!*" James takes a step back, almost scuffing Lexington's shoes. "Now, you know that's my favorite, right? Don't disappoint me."

"I think you will enjoy them."

"Then, I will see you tomorrow." James turns around to a seething Lexington. "What's up, Lex? Nice suit."

James walks back outside.

"Clearly, he wasn't raised with any manners," Lexington huffs while adjusting his cuffs. "Anyway, back to our conversation–"

"Listen, Lex, I don't want this conversation going any further than it needs to." She places her hand on his shoulder. "I'm happy for you with your test results, okay? So, let's leave it at that and you have yourself a good afternoon."

Cadina pats his shoulder like an old chum and trots up the staircase.

Watching the way her ponytail bounces off her back, he suppresses the thought of yanking her ass back down those stairs.

Bitch, you ain't the only fish in the sea.

DAVENPORT

Tap...Tap...Tap...Tap...Tap...
Lounging behind his desk, Davenport subconsciously beats his pen to the cadence of the clock that ticks the afternoon seconds away. He is a bit ticked off himself. Rising from his desk, the manager rubs his head as he stands in front of the big calendar on the wall. Earlier, he received a call from midtown informing him that Sterling's status has been upgraded to managing another station for an indefinite amount of time.

He knew this was going to happen.

Still, he does not find it too pleasing that the powers-to-be would disrupt the mechanical rhythms of his reputable station without sending a competent supervisor who would possess half of Sterling's caliber to replace him. Somebody who could monitor all the truck routes without the chaos, run the computer operation, and relate to the carriers while simultaneously earning their respect. That's the person they're taking away from Davenport. The sheer thought of a 'wet-behind-the-ears' supervisor coming straight from the academy and into his station provokes him to rub his head even more.

Tucker breezes into the office with a song and two-step dance shuffle.

"*We're gonna have a gooood time tonight! Let's celebrate...it's alright!* Be the background vocals for me, Michael..."

He manages a weary grin at Tucker who, with her dreadlocks twirling around in the air, has every reason to be jovial.

Tucker stops dancing. She leans on the desk and then clasps her hands. "Come on, Michael. It was bound to happen sooner or later. Sterling has been in this profession almost as long as you have, and I wouldn't be too surprised if he accepts the job permanently."

"I know." Davenport circles around his desk and plops back in his seat. "But can I be selfish for once? Shoot, I mean, I had the perfect staff in place. The better the staff, the better the numbers look in the long run. I live and die by that mantra."

"Will you put your numbers to the side and focus on Lexington?"

He finally cracks a smile. "He damn near aced that test. A *ninety-eight* percent?!?"

"So you *have* heard about it!"

"I got the call about an hour ago."

"Our boy topped them all!" Tucker rejoices by pumping a fist in the air. "Oh, and he also did a good job today in front of the panel, as well."

Davenport raises an eyebrow. "You heard about that already?"

"I sure have. They confided in me that he was a little green in certain areas of the interview, but overall, they said he did an exceptional job and carried himself like a true professional."

"That is good news."

"Now, where are we treating him because I'm ready to eat!"

"Let's go to the Sugar Bar uptown. They have live music, plus the food is incredible."

"Sounds good to me. I'll tell the future supervisor." Tucker retrieves her coat and briefcase. "Oh yeah, one more thing..."

"What's that?"

"*We're gonna have a gooood time tonight! Let's celebrate! It's alright!* That's okay. I'll be my own background chorus. *Ceeeeeelebraaation time, come on!*"

She dances her way out of the office.

The room is quiet again.

Davenport's brooding picks up where it left off.

Then out of nowhere, an idea overwhelms him, causing him to quickly grab the phone and dial a number.

He waits.

The receptionist answers.

"Yes, is Elgin in?" he asks. "Tell him it's Michael...yes, I'll hold... Elgin? Hey...man, I can't call it...oh, yes, I'll be at the Knicks game tomorrow...listen, I'm in a bit of a bind and hopefully you can help me out...his name is Lexington VanGuard..." Davenport grins. "My man..."

Failing to understand why he didn't think of it sooner, Davenport starts to tap his pen even faster.

Tap,tap,tap,tap,tap,tap,tap,tap....

———◦———

"And what can I get for you, Sir?"

Davenport slides his glasses on before reading the menu. "I'll have the grilled jerk pork chops with ahhh, let's see here, oh, collard greens and mac and cheese, thank you."

"You're welcome. Will there be anything else?"

"Some more yeast rolls, please, thank you," Lexington says, eyeing the cute waitress.

"You're quite welcome."

She cheerfully takes the menus and returns Lexington's stare before leaving.

The men stretch their necks to watch the sonic movement of her bubble butt bounce all the way back to the restaurant's kitchen.

"When she comes back out, try closing your mouths, please, it's just way too obvious," jibes Tucker.

They all laugh.

Lexington continues. "...like I was saying, when the third panelist asked me what the number one goal of a supervisor was, and I said, '*keeping the carriers' overtime hours to a minimum,*' you should have seen the look on their faces!"

Davenport smiles and then says, "They were impressed, huh?"

"That or they knew I was coached well by you. Either way, I got the job done."

"I heard that."

The waitress returns with a platter full of drinks and yeast rolls. "Be careful with the rolls, they're pretty warm."

"They're not the only thing that's pretty around here." Lexington coyly smiles at her.

"You must be having a wonderful day today."

"Actually, I am. You're just adding to it."

The waitress blushes. "Your food will be out shortly. Can I get y'all anything else?"

Davenport and Tucker say no.

"What about you, Mr. Happy?"

"I'm good, thanks."

"Okay. I'll go check on your food."

She gives Lexington a lingering gaze before returning to the kitchen.

"My man is batting a thousand today!" Davenport nudges his shoulder.

Lexington leans back in his chair. "Whoo, she is *fine*."

"Both of y'all hush while I make a toast," Tucker says.

The trio raises their drinks.

"To Lexington, as he sets forth to excel in management. Allow the advanced knowledge you're about to acquire from the Academy to become the beacon of light that will enable you to help others succeed in their journeys, as well. Cheers..."

"Cheers!"

Ting!

Davenport takes a sip of his whiskey ginger and then clears his throat. "My sources told me an unusual amount of people took that exam yesterday."

"Man, there were so many people." Lexington butters one of the rolls. "I even heard one of the examiners say they may hold two separate classes if the majority of the people that took the test passed."

"That person was correct. The first class will be given in a couple of weeks while the second class will take place during the summer."

"Hey, as long as I'm in the first class, I'm good. I'm ready to leave Midway, like right now."

"I'm afraid you're in that second class, Lex."

Tucker and Lexington stop drinking.

Tucker turns to Davenport, confused. "Did I hear you clearly, Michael?"

"Yes, you did."

"Hold on now. I didn't make the first class?" Lexington asks, with equal perplexity. "How can that be?"

"When did you hear about this, Michael?" Tucker quizzed.

Davenport wipes his mouth with a napkin. "Right before you came in the office announcing his test score."

"But why didn't you mention this to me then?"

Davenport laughs. "You never gave me the chance! You danced into my office, we spoke briefly about his test results, and then you danced right back out! It probably slipped my mind, I'm sorry."

"But I got a *ninety-eight*." Lexington places his drink on the table. "I thought I'd be the *first* one to be slotted in the first class since I scored so high."

"The one area the program is focusing on right now is effective leadership skills. The people chosen for the first class have prior knowledge in the managerial and supervisory fields. You said it yourself, Denise, the board felt he was a little green in certain areas of their questioning."

"*Green?*" Lexington repeats. "What did they mean by that?"

"It means that by the way you answered your questions, the panel knew you weren't seasoned enough in supervision," Tucker explains before turning back to Davenport. "But I also said he did an exceptional job overall before the panel."

"You're making it seem like it was my doing, Denise." Davenport stirs his drink with a straw. "This is something they implemented as a priority because of the enormous amount of people that passed. I can't change that."

"I see you're taking this bit of news rather comfortably. *Too* comfortable for my taste."

"*Denise*, what do you want me to do?" Davenport sips his whiskey. "Rules are rules."

"Correct me if I'm wrong, Michael, but if they claimed he was exceptional and scored damn near a hundred on the exam...I don't know, I just see things a lot differently than you."

"Damn." Lexington now sulks in his seat. "And I was so ready to go *now*."

Davenport breaks into a gut-busting howl. "You two act like I just announced a death sentence. Did y'all forget why we're here in the first place? You made it, son!"

"Well, I just didn't think my departure would be prolonged."

"Well, since it has, I'm not going to waste any time promoting you to permanent 204B Acting Supervisor." Davenport inches closer to Lexington. "And with the proper guidance from our staff, you will be able to leave Midway altogether with supreme confidence in your advanced abilities. Now, how does that sound to you?"

Lexington sighs. "Well, if that's the road I have to take, I have no other choice, right?"

"Good, then it's settled."

The waitress arrives with their entrées.

As she places a sizzling plate in front of each person, she smiles and asks, "Do y'all want me to bring out more rolls?"

"Yes indeed, young lady!" Davenport claps. "They are definitely scrumptious!"

"Aren't they?" The waitress turns to Lexington. "What about you, Mr. Happy? You need me to bring you anything else?"

"Uh, no, I'm good, thanks."

"Are you *sure*?"

"I *said* I'm good, alright?" he snaps. "Thank you."

The waitress stops smiling.

Embarrassed, she manages to maintain her professional manner. "Okay, um, I'll be back with more rolls." She half-smiles at the managers and then shoots Lexington a confused look before walking off towards the back.

Tucker slowly picks at her grilled salmon.

Lexington doesn't touch his catfish plate.

Davenport leans in closer to his prized pupil. "If I were you, I wouldn't leave here without her phone number."

Davenport roars into laughter as he tears into his piping hot pork chop.

LEXINGTON

*L*exington stands in front of his letter case, still processing the unexpected news he received the previous evening. The ball of confusion nestled inside his throat stands out like a swollen Adam's apple. He just knew he was about to kiss this station goodbye. Now he must suck it up for another five months. Five *long* months. He snaps out of his funk when Chapman walks over to him with his hand extended.

"I believe a congratulation is in order."

Lexington shakes his hand. "Thanks. I guess I won't be cleaning out my locker any time soon."

"Awww, you'll be fine. The second class will be here before you know it and you'll be well on your way."

"That day can't come quick enough if you ask me." He ponders for a moment. "You know, I only did the acting supervisor role twice here, but both times these people wanted to jump down my throat every time I gave them instructions. How do you maintain your composure when they come at you like that?"

"Good question." Chapman mulls for a moment. "Three things; one, everybody is not going to always agree with you, so stand firm with your decisions. Two, don't take any work-related stress home with you. And lastly, have integrity, especially when you make a mistake, and you will make some…we all do, but own up to them and move on. I was a carrier many moons ago before making the transition, so they're going to test you, there's no denying that. But if you stay consistent with those three things, you should fare well."

Lexington nods. "Appreciate it."

"And since this is your last day in a carrier uniform, how about doing me one last favor?"

"Who do you want me to bail out now?"

"Cadina. She's on Marc's route again and she will need all the help she can get."

The mere mention of her name sends angry ripples throughout his being. At this point, he does not care to do *anything* for that stuck-up broad, but he keeps that to himself.

He fakes a smile. "Yeah, I'll help her out."

"Thanks. Lunch is on me today."

Chapman pats him on the back before returning to the podium.

Lexington leans back on the ledge for a moment. As much as he hates to admit it, Davenport was right. These next few months are going to be very crucial for him to get his leadership skills up to par.

He finally mans up.

If Chapman can deal with these people, so can I. I'll show them. I'll show them ALL what I'm really made of. Yeah, the next five months are mine to conquer!

Cadina catches his eye.

He watches as she helps the mail-handler give out the mail.

Out of nowhere, James enters the scene. He pulls out his wallet and shows Cadina what seems to be a photo. They both laugh. James slides the photo back into his wallet and walks to his workstation. Cadina continues to smile as she resumes handing out the mail.

Jealousy grabs him by the jugular.

Yeah, I'll help her out. But I got a trick for that ass, though.

He swings back around to case the letters, with resentment flooding his eyes.

CADINA

*C*adina slams the mailbox panel shut and locks it. She gathers all the returned letters from the brownstone's hallway table and walks outside to release a sigh of relief.

She is finished for the day.

Observing the sun beating down on the pavement produces a smile across her face. The last time she finished this early was when she first started. Some of her coworkers have amusingly labeled her as the station's current nocturnal carrier, which doesn't really bother her. However, feeling the afternoon sun rays upon her wintered face is a welcomed change from her normal routine.

Pushing her mailcart down the sidewalk, she reflects on her catering dilemma. Somehow, she has convinced herself that taking tomorrow off will not hurt anybody and that she'd never do it again.

Old habits die hard.

She pulls out her phone to call her mother. It rings four times before she answers.

"Hey, girl, what's up?"

"Nothing much. How long have you been home?"

"I just walked in the door. Why?"

"I'm about to clock out in a half-hour and when I get home, I want us to go grocery shopping."

"I see you're having an early day today, that's good."

"It's about time. And it couldn't have fallen on a better day."

"You mean with Bianca's surprise party tomorrow and all..."

"Exactly."

"I know you're glad they gave you the day off, right?"

"Uh, yeah, right."

Guilt does not begin to describe how she feels lying to her mother about having permission to take this Saturday off. But she could live with that for right now. "Did you see the list I left on the fridge?"

"Didn't I tell you I just walked in the house?"

"My bad, jeez."

Cadina stops at the corner on Seventh Street.

She happens to glance at the relay box and notices long relay bag strings hanging from outside its door. Curious, she opens the relay box door and sees four stuffed relay bags she had left for Lexington to deliver.

"Bianca *did* give you the money to buy all of this food, right?" Lorraine asks. "My Lord, she has you cooking for an army!"

"That's what I'm known for, remember? Let me call you back, okay?"

"Call me when you're on your way home, bye."

Cadina ends the call and then speed-dials her station.

Chapman answers the phone.

"Midway Station, Mr. Chapman speaking, may I help you?"

"Hey, It's Cadina. Look, I don't know if you need to be concerned with this, but Lex—"

"Cadina! I'm so glad you called. Listen, Lex came back to the station feeling a bit under the weather, so he went home. I need you to get started on those bags right away and I'll try to send the next available body out there to give you a hand, okay?"

A ton of bricks just rained on her parade.

"Are you *serious*?"

"I wish I wasn't, but I can't have those bags just sitting out there without getting delivered."

"Well, how long will it take for someone else to arrive?" She hastily checks her watch.

"I can't tell you off-hand, but someone will be sent out there to assist you, okay? I have another call to take, call me if you run into any problems, okay? Thanks."

"But, Mr. Chapman-"

Click!

"Shit!"

Cadina stands in front of the relay box, stunned. Those four relay bags equal out to two more hours at the very least! She did not expect karma to catch up to her this quickly. Chewing on her bottom lip, she contemplates her next move when a wrinkled hand taps her on the shoulder.

"Excuse me, young lady..."

She turns around to a troll-sized elderly woman wearing a multi-colored headscarf and a smelly brown wool coat. Her rubbery, squinted face resembles a Party City Halloween mask.

"May I help you, Ma'am?"

Leaning on her cane, the elderly woman says in a creaky voice, "All day long, I've been watching you walk up and down the other side of the street delivering mail, and you act like you're in no hurry to deliver to this side of the block and I've been waiting patiently for my social security check so I can get it cashed. Where is Marc, anyway?"

"He fell sick today, so he stayed home."

"And *you're* his replacement?" the snaggletooth woman snarls, as she pointed a finger that displayed a seashell-thick fingernail. "You better start getting here a little earlier or I'm gonna call your station and report you!"

Trembling with frustration, Cadina says, "Look Ma'am, I'm not the only person that's going to be covering this route—"

"Find my fuckin' check so I can cash it, please!"

The elderly woman plants a wad of Big Red tobacco inside the cheek of her mouth and begins chewing on it like a bulldog.

"What's your name and address?" Cadina asks.

The elderly woman spits out some of the chewed tobacco juice on the sidewalk and says, "Agatha Concepcion. I live right across the street, in the garden apartment. Here's my identification."

"Thank you, but I can't just hand you the mail out in the open. I have to deliver it to your mailbox, or I'd get in trouble—"

"Well, then stop your fuckin' babbling and meet me across the street, *now*! The check-cashing place closes in five minutes!"

She spits out some more tobacco juice before hobbling back across the street.

Searching for the relay bag with Agatha's mail in it, Cadina wishes for her help to arrive soon before she winds up spraying a few curse words of her own towards the tobacco-chewing hag.

Six-thirty in the evening; her usual clocking out period.

After promising James for the fourth time that she will be at his housewarming tomorrow evening, she exits the station and drags her dog-tired body down Eleventh Street en route to the subway station.

Still upset over the afternoon's events, it did, however, cement her decision to take tomorrow off. She has so much to do and so little time to do it in. She is used to cooking under stressful situations, but the playing field is much different this time around. Her body is exhausted from a week of driving trucks and slinging heavy bags all over town. She reminds herself to get at least a couple of hours of sleep after she food-shops with her mother, or else she will be dead on her feet come tomorrow morning. The challenge is on.

Cadina turns the corner of Fourth Avenue and spots Velour, dressed in a cream-colored biker jacket over a cream-colored jumpsuit, conversing on her phone. The postal diva leans on a sparkling pearl-white Porsche.

They trade smiles.

"I'll talk to you later, okay, bye." Velour slides the phone in her Gucci pocketbook. "Hey, Boo."

"Hey." Cadina's eyes are glued to the gleaming vehicle. "Is this you?"

"Two thousand sixteen Porsche Cayenne Turbo S–premium package," Velour boasts. "A gift to *moi*."

"An expensive gift, at that."

"Price tags don't scare me." Velour presses a remote button to roll down the Porsche's windows. She places her purse in the passenger seat. "Once I claim something, it's already mine, trust. I see you had another long day."

Cadina sighs, "I don't even wanna talk about it."

Velour chuckles. "You're going to have plenty of days like this, Boo, so my advice to you is to take it with a grain of salt and make that money. And, just maybe, in a few years, you can have yourself one of these."

Velour pats her shiny vehicle to emphasize her point.

"Yeah, right. Heading home?"

"Nope. I'm going to buy this fierce outfit I saw on Broadway for James' housewarming. Best believe I'm going to shut that party down tomorrow, you watch."

Cadina laughs. "It's just a housewarming party, Velour."

"Honey, I have standards to uphold. I just can't be looking any old kind of way out in public. I have to present myself accordingly."

"See, that's what I admire about you."

"What do you admire about me, girl?"

"I don't know, you seem to have this fearless attitude towards life. It can be very contagious."

Velour blushes at this admiration. She moves in closer to Cadina. "Like my brother always told me when we were young; if you're willing to work hard in life, you should be able to play twice as hard. And as of right now, life is a playground."

Cadina nods. "I heard that."

"See you tomorrow, Cadina."

Velour backpedals to her Porsche, slides behind the wheel, cranks up Lil' Kim's, *No Time For Fake Ones,* and peels off in dramatic fashion.

Cadina begins walking down the street while taking mental notes.

She's definitely raking in the dough...

Her phone rings.

It's her mother.

Ah, man...

She swipes her phone and says, "I know, Ma-"

"You said you'd be home two hours ago. What happened?"

"I'm sorry I didn't call you back, but I'll explain everything when we go shopping."

"Well, I'ma head out now, because you need to get some rest as soon as you get home."

"I'll be fine, Ma. But make sure you grab the list that I put on the fridge and I will meet you at the supermarket..."

Cadina heads down the subway stairs.

TUCKER

Something is not right. She feels it in her bones.
Saturday morning and the assistant manager, with her briefcase in one hand and coffee in the other, rides the elevator to the work floor. While taking a sip, her brain tries to decipher the situation involving Lexington's postponed enrollment. The timing of the whole matter is what disturbs her the most. Why didn't Davenport inform her about the added second class prior to the celebration dinner, so she would not have appeared just as surprised as Lexington when the subject was brought up? Or was it his intention to withhold that bit of information from her until the dinner? If so, *why*? They never operated under those conditions before.

Davenport has never given her a reason to doubt his credibility on any subject and up until now, he has always been sincere about his straightforwardness. Still, she has never been one to push a nagging feeling over to the sidelines. Tackling the bull by its horns is in her genetic structure, so she intends to find out whether this matter is legit, even if it means going over his head to do it.

She arrives on the work floor, greets the mail clerks, and checks the call-in sheet to see if anyone has called in absent.

One name sticks out like a sore thumb.

She cannot believe her eyes.

She *refuses* to believe her eyes.

Tucker turns to the clerk supervisor. "Excuse me, Barry, do you know who took Cadina's phone call?"

"Oh, she called right before you came in," he answers while condensing a letter tray.

"And what did she say?"

Barry shrugs. "Well, she told me she was coming down with the twenty-four-hour flu bug and she couldn't make it in."

No, she didn't! "Thanks."

She tosses her empty cup in a nearby wastebasket and storms back downstairs to her office.

CADINA

She manages to jolt herself out of a nap and race into the kitchen. She snatches the oven door open, pulls out two pans to inspect her Creole honey barbeque ribs, and breathes a huge sigh of relief. She curses herself for nodding off after she called the station, but her body was on the brink of shutting down hours ago. She pushes the pan back into the oven to let it brown some more.

She plops down in a dinette chair and gradually browses over all the prepared dishes made within the past sixteen hours. It was on pure adrenaline alone that she accomplished her mission without a wink of sleep. She grabs the house phone to call her sister, who answers on one ring.

"Girl, I was just about to call you," Camille says.

"I hope you didn't make any plans today because I'ma need you to transport a lot of this food to the function, so you can start making space in the back of your Yukon and what time are you gonna try to make it over here because— "

"Whoa, whoa, whoa! Good God! Mom did say you were up all night, so I'm going to excuse the tone in your voice."

"I'm sorry. Just a little burnt out."

"Just a little, huh? What time is the party?"

"At three o'clock, in Bed-Stuy. You know where Cornerstone Baptist Church is, right? Right on Lewis and Madison?"

"Yes, Cadina, I do. Another question: did you remember to get the disposable chafing kits to keep the food warm?"

"*Shit!* I knew I forgot something!"

"Wow, okay. But did you design menus?"

"They didn't ask me to provide menus, Cammy, they just wanted me to prepare the food. That was it."

"Girl, they didn't have to ask you, this is about *your* presentation. Ms. Pauline is a wealthy angel investor, am I correct?"

Cadina rolls her eyes. "Yes, you are. And?"

"*And*, you're about to cater to a group of upper-class people who will be taking mental notes of you and your services. *And*, I'm quite sure there's going to be networking opportunities so everything has to be top-notch in order to attract future clients, come on now, girl."

This is the one thing their father adores about Camille; her entrepreneurial spirit.

Cadina hears a beep on the line. "Hold on for a sec, someone's beeping in." She presses the flash button. "Hello?"

"Good morning, my name is Denise Tucker, the assistant manager of Mid…Is this Cadina?"

She drops the phone.

Fear has frozen her body solid.

Oh, my God!

Tucker called her bluff big time.

She did not think her boss was even allowed, or bold enough for that matter, to call the house to check up on her. She thought wrong.

In slow motion, she retrieves the handset from the floor and nearly jumps to the ceiling when the phone rings in her hand. She checks the Caller I.D. before answering. It's her sister.

Cadina blows out relief. "Hey."

"What happened?"

"Uh, somehow we got disconnected when I switched over. Listen, could you be a doll and buy the kits and I reimburse you? I finally finished cooking and right now, I need to shut it all the way down."

"I gotcha. And before you do that, text me a list of the food you made, and I'll print out a batch of fancy menus. Shoot, my sister is not going out like no punk!"

"What will I ever do without you?"

"Hey, you need someone in your corner that's going to help mold you into that future entrepreneur."

"Now, you already know I have a full-time job."

"Yes, I do and it's the *wrong* full-time job. Get some rest, Boo."

Camille hangs up.

Cadina checks on her ribs. Pleased with the taste, she takes both pans out of the oven and wraps foil over them.

The phone rings.

She checks the number.

It's Tucker again.

She quickly turns the answering machine off.

She does not want Tucker leaving any messages she might not want to hear later. The phone continues to ring. And ring. And ring four more times before stopping altogether. Cadina's mind begins to play its customary tricks again.

But she doesn't really know it was me, it could've been my sister answering the phone in her sleep. Yeah, that's it!

Gradually coming to terms with her future alibi, she places both pans of ribs in the box marked MEAT and then teeters to her bedroom for some much-needed shut-eye.

Five o'clock in the afternoon and the Cornerstone Baptist Church Center is thunderously raising the roof in gospel jubilee. After stomping along with Kirk Franklin's music, Cadina and Camille slither their way through the praising and worshipping crowd to a pair of vacant folding chairs along the side of the wall.

Camille fans the top of her black dress to allow her bosom to get some air. "Girl, if one more person asks for a plate of food, I'm going to cuss, you hear me?"

Cadina, also dressed in black, playfully grabs her sister's chin. "And after you finish cursing, you're going to serve that guest with that beautiful smile of yours."

"You better be glad I closed up my shop to help you out. Everything turned out great!"

"Didn't it?"

Cadina cannot help but smile.

Everyone who attended the event, young and old, devoured practically everything they placed on the dinner tables. Even with the requested second helpings, she and Camille found themselves rushing back and forth from the kitchen to the patiently, yet eagerly awaiting, attendees who left no bones or crumbs to be desired. From the zesty beef ribs dipped in her own secret Creole barbeque sauce to her baked ziti—*Gone*. Grilled salmon, baked catfish, baked and fried chicken—*Bye-Bye*. Yams, potato salad, collard greens, sweet onion and sweet pea mixed vegetable dish, tossed salad, deviled eggs—*See ya!* Even the 'Wah-co' taco salad dish she'd been experimenting with and perfected the past week—*Peace!*

But what really touched her heart was when people would pass her their business cards or pull her to the side to discuss employing her for future affairs. And it had as much to do with the added extras as it did the food. People loved the menus her sister designed which honored the birthday lady, the small bags of miniature chocolates, and the other festive trinkets which were placed at each table. Prior to the event, Cadina caught the brainstorm bug and jetted to Party City to buy a top hat and horn for the birthday lady. All and all, she was extremely pleased with the way things turned out.

Camille suddenly stands. "Here comes Bianca with the birthday girl."

Cadina rises to her feet as well.

Dressed in a gold blazer, a black medium-length skirt, and a joyful expression is Bianca, who works her way over to the sisters. By her side, wearing the top hat that Cadina bought and blowing the horn is Bianca's mother, Pauline. Everyone embraces one another.

"Ma'am, all I want to say is you're my role model," Camille says, holding Pauline's bracelet-adorned arm. "You look fabulous!"

Laced in a two-piece leopard-printed pants suit, with gold high-heels to match her short, blond hair, the brown-skinned birthday diva strikes an 'en vogue' pose.

"Child, tell me something I don't know!" Pauline blows her horn and laughs a deep, baritone laugh. She then turns to Cadina. "Cadina, Cadina, Cadina. I have one question to ask you, my dear..."

"Yes, Ma'am."

"Where did you learn how to prepare so many wonderful dishes? Child, I'm still farting out those collard greens you made, they were so *tasty*—"

"Motherrrr..." Bianca covers her face in embarrassment. "Too much information!"

"Oh, hush," Pauline waves her off. "I'm just letting her know she did an amazing job. Now, how long have you been in the catering business?"

Cadina feels giddy. "To answer your first question, our mother taught us how to cook at an early age, and I just kind of gravitated towards it. As for catering, I don't do this for a living, but once Bianca asked if I could cater your birthday, I felt honored to do so."

Pauline studies Cadina's face. "Hmmm. I see we're going to have to do something about that in the future, my dear."

Cadina grabs Camille's arm. "And my beautiful sister helped me with the decorative features and menus; so, it was a collaborative effort."

Pauline cups both hands together and points at the sisters. "Both of you, for making my day so extravagant, I will be forever grateful. Now, if y'all will excuse me, I must get my boogie on. Ain't God good?"

The birthday diva once again blows her horn, tips her top hat at everyone, and sashays across the thumping dance floor.

Bianca turns around and gives the sisters a hug. "Thank you both so much! I'll call you when it's time to cut the cake!"

Bianca leaves to entertain the other guests.

The sisters return to their seats.

Cadina checks her watch. "I hope the party ends on time so I can get ready for my next event."

"Yes! This housewarming gathering you've been invited to," Camille smirks. "What's his name and why does he get to have a big pan of oxtails when I've been begging you for the past three months to make me some?"

Cadina holds back a big grin. "Well, his name is James Richards. He works at my station. He and his mother just moved into their first home. He seems really cool."

"Any kids?"

"A daughter. I met his family the other day."

Cadina catches the worrisome expression on her sister's face.

"Now, you know how Pops feel about you fraternizing and you just started the job-"

"What, now I can't have any friends? I didn't say I was going to marry the guy-"

"I'm just saying. Don't let Pop find out."

"And if he did, he'd be alright. He can't run my life forever, I'm a grown woman-"

"You're just as stubborn as the day is long. And you're going to give me some of those oxtails before you take them to that party."

Cadina laughs. "Okay, okay. But just one scoop."

"Uh, uh. You are not monitoring my scoops, girl!"

Two gentlemen walk up to the ladies. They both appear to be in their fifties. And they both have that look of lust in their eyes.

"Excuse us, but, uh, we know you two have been busy all day serving folks," the taller gentleman says, quickly glancing at his friend. "But we were wondering if we can squeeze just one dance out of y'all before the evening is over with?"

"Yes, *Lord*," His friend adds, eyeballing Camille's bosom.

The sisters stare at the men before turning to each other, trying hard not to laugh.

Camille takes the lead as she stands.

"Okay, but I'm letting you both know right now that's the only thing you two are *squeezing* out of us, I hope I'm making myself clear-"

"Oh, yes, Ma'am!" the taller gentleman offers his hand to Cadina.

Cadina respectfully smiles as she takes the gentleman's hand and allows him to take her to the packed dance floor.

DAVENPORT

Davenport strolls inside of the nearly vacant station and heads straight to his office. Tucker had called him earlier while he was shopping in the SoHo district nearby. She was still scalding-hot about Cadina calling in sick earlier that morning. Mentioning that she wanted to fire the new sub on the spot once she arrives Monday morning, prompted him to now have to make an urgent trip to the station on what would have been his day off.

His assistant manager, as well as his dear friend, is known for using her energy to help employees keep their jobs rather than terminating them. And he does not see anything remotely different in Cadina's case, especially since her work performance has proved beyond exceptional since her first day on the job.

No, he senses something more...*Much* more.

Tucker has been somewhat distant toward him ever since that celebration dinner at the Sugar Bar. Her eyes threw silent darts at him all day yesterday and she never once said what was on her mind.

She's on to him.

They know each other like a book, footnotes and all. But if she were to skim through some of the additional pages he has recently tacked on, she would be surprised at what she would find. And if she has uncovered them already, well, he hopes she is willing to ride along with the current waves, instead of trying to confront them, as things could get a bit ugly.

He enters his office and sees Tucker in the corner, clicking away on the computer. Quietly, he removes his jacket and hat, hanging them on the coat stand. He then clears his throat for no reason and sits behind his desk to look over the numbers for the day. Not a word is spoken between the two of them.

"What time did the last carrier clock out?" he asks, breaking the silence.

"Around four-thirty."

He glances at the clock—5:15 pm. "You had yourself a good day then."

She continues tapping on the keyboard buttons without saying a word.

"So...are you attending James' party tonight?"

"Planning on it."

Her answers are short and to the point.

That's not her style at all.

He strolls over to sit on a short file cabinet right next to where she is working.

"I see Cadina got you all riled up to the point where you want to fire her? This doesn't sound like the Denise I know."

Tucker stops typing. She swivels her chair in his direction.

He gazes into her skeptical eyes.

She wears them like reading glasses.

He braces himself.

"Apparently, you don't know anything about the little prelude we had earlier in the week which led to her calling in sick this morning, so let me fill you in."

"By all means."

She stands and begins pacing the floor. "This past Tuesday, Cadina asked to have today off and I told her we couldn't do it because she's on probation, plus she was scheduled on a truck assignment. She *told* me she understood. But why do I come in this morning and see her name at the top of the call-in sheet? I knew damn well she wasn't sick, so I called her home, and do you know she had the audacity to hang up on me? I mean, who does that?"

Davenport grunts, now understanding the true nature of her fury.

"Do you know what she's saying to me by pulling this stunt, Michael? *The hell with you, Mrs. Tucker! I'm takin' the day off, regardless of your orders!* I swear, I could just—ugh!"

He chuckles. "You know, this is the first time I've ever seen you this upset over an employee's insubordination."

"Well, maybe if I were a little more dogmatic, people would think twice about testing my authority. I mean, am I wrong, Michael?"

"No, no. I'll back you one hundred percent if you feel there's no other way to resolve this matter."

Tucker sighs as she drops down in her seat. "I spoke to her father this afternoon."

"You have?" He raises an eyebrow. "How did that go?"

"I told him what happened and what I was planning to do about it. Michael, this man begged and pleaded his daughter's case, saying she'll never do it again. Long story short—"

"You gave in."

"She gets one more chance, Michael. I told her father if she doesn't get her act together, she's outta here, no third chances."

She swivels her chair back around to the computer.

Davenport chuckles as he walks across the office to retrieve his trench coat and hat.

"I would love to be a fly on James' wall when you two meet up tonight."

"Well, it's a risk she's going to have to take. I'm going to enjoy myself tonight."

"I heard that. Give my regards to James and his family."

"Where are you going?"

He opens the door. "To pick up Brenda from the nail salon and grab something to eat. You want to join us?"

"Close the door. We need to talk."

"Everything okay?"

Tucker swivels her chair back around. She crosses her arms. "I spoke to Elgin this afternoon, Michael."

His smile vanishes.

He calmly closes the door and takes off his hat and coat. He circles back behind his desk, only for the added authority that may be required during the debate that they are about to dive into. He sits down, crosses his legs, and says in a very calm manner, "I'm listening."

"We had a very interesting discussion regarding Lexington's situation. I brought it to his attention because it was gnawing at my own curiosity."

He taps his fingers on the desk. "And?"

"Did you have *anything* to do with switching Lexington's classes?"

He directs his devious grin down toward the desk.

She shakes her head in disgust. "Michael, how *could* you?"

"I would've told you soon enough-"

"You know, between you, Freeman and Cadina...the three of you must think I'm some new type of fool in this station-"

"On the contrary, Denise; I value you, completely." He leans back in his chair. "That's why I selected you as my assistant manager. But as far as this situation goes, you can spare me the dramatics, especially when there is no need for it."

"Who the hell gave *you* the authority to play chess with that man's career? And please don't tell me this has something to do with Sterling leaving the station, either."

Davenport stands. "Think about it, Denise. Having Lexington here will benefit him and the station long term. He's excellent with our computer system, he knows the logistics of all the routes, plus he has the kind of temperament that's necessary for dealing with some of the more rebellious carriers in the station-"

"But you're making it *his* problem to shoulder and that's not fair at all! That man has earned the right to move on to his next location-"

"And he *will*, Denise. Later this year."

"If you're so gung-ho about this pet project of yours, why not share it with the man who idolizes you instead of lying to his face as if you had absolutely nothing to do with this?"

Davenport felt the sting of that comeback.

But he plays it off coolly.

"What he doesn't know won't hurt him."

"Oh, really?" Tucker stands. "Well, *I* know. And it can be easily undone when the E. E. O. Commissions *and* the Carriers' Union Delegates catch wind of your little self-serving project."

"You're threatening *me*, Denise?" He laughs out loud. "In my office? Wow."

"I don't dish out threats, Michael, those are promises I'm making."

"You know what? Since you're so adamant about what *I'm* doing behind closed doors, let's talk about a particular situation you tried to keep from me a few weeks back."

"What situation?"

"You know exactly what I'm referring to, Denise; Freeman's accident."

Her bravado melts away, instantly.

He anticipated this happening.

He did not want to pull out the big guns on her just yet, but he had no choice in the matter since she went behind his back and pulled one of his cards.

He pours it on.

"Now, did I come to you and say you were being self-serving by withholding Freeman's true condition the day of the accident? Come to think of it, were you ever going to fill me in on that negligence?"

Tightlipped, she manages to squeeze out, "Freeman is not the issue here—"

"See! You weren't going to tell me! Why? Because you took it upon yourself to deal with the situation privately! You didn't need for me to worry about it, just like I don't need you badgering me about Lexington's situation-"

"But the difference here is I was helping Freeman with his dilemma! You, on the other hand, are hindering Lexington's forward progress and that's outright cruel and thoughtless on your part—"

"Bullshit. You were more worried about covering your own ass than helping Freeman—who do you think you're fooling here? You *knew* you were in the wrong for letting that man drive in his condition, but you did it anyway!"

"I-I know what I did, Michael. And for the record, he was not drunk-"

"He was *hungover*, Denise! Which is just as bad, you know this! And suppose that accident was his fault, what do you think would've happened next? Huh? The Postmaster would've held *you* responsible and you'd be fighting for your job as we speak! And *had* that happened, I would've fought for you because that's what we managers do. You, my dear, better get used to how the game is played at this level or you're going to find yourself fighting losing battles, *alone*."

His penetrating speech leaves her vocally impaired and visibly stunned.

She breaks out of that spell by shutting down the computer, throwing her coat on, and wrapping her scarf around her dreads. All in humiliated silence.

"Denise, all I'm asking is for your support as a manager of this station because you know I'd do the same for you."

Tucker swings the door open. "Have a good afternoon, Michael."

"Denise-"

SLAM!

The portraits on the wall rattle in response to Tucker's anger.

Damn.

He was victorious in their battle, but there is no cause for celebrating. Relief would be his only reward. Never in his life could he imagine hurting one of his closest friends. But no one is going to change the way he runs Midway. Not even one who is as kind and generous as Denise.

His phone vibrates in his pocket.

It's his wife, Brenda.

He swipes his phone and says, "Hey, are you ready? Yes, I'm leaving the office now...But we already had seafood yesterday...My taste buds are calling for barbeque...No, I'm not being selfish."

He laughs as he slides on his coat. He turns off the lights and closes the door behind him.

JAMES

"**H**OT WINGS OVER HERE!" James shouts, entering the festive living room of his new home, carrying a steaming platter of wings that his mother prepared.

His cousin Sabrina dances over to him and takes the platter from his hands. She yells out over the music, "IS THE LASAGNA READY?"

"I'MA BRING IT OUT IN A MINUTE!"

"YOU BETTER HURRY UP! PEOPLE HUNGRY UP IN HERE!"

"I KNOW, I KNOW!"

Hands from every direction snatch up a wing or two as Sabrina dances the platter over to the food table.

James stands in the middle of the swinging doorway. He takes in the moment.

Now, this is what I'm talkin' about.

His dream home, finally a reality. Three spacious bedrooms—an eat-in kitchen; huge living and dining room areas; no more waiting in line to use one bathroom—they now possess two full bathrooms and a half; a sizable basement which he furnished as a man cave; a two-car garage; a wide front porch, and a decent-size backyard just screaming for summertime grilling.

Nineteen hundred square feet of pure bliss.

His eyes moisten.

Surveying the living room, it fills his heart to see family and friends enjoy themselves at his housewarming. On one side of the room, his cousin Sabrina, her female companions, and his aunts engage in loud girl-talk over appetizers. Across from them, Divine and

Tucker's husband, Elliott, battle another couple in spades. James' male cousins, uncles, and the postal crew congregate in the dining room to watch the Knicks on his seventy-five-inch flat-screen. Some folks are eating, others are dancing and some doing both.

Life couldn't get any better.

Apart from Cadina showing up.

He hears commotion at the deejay table.

Both Shabbazz, the evening's deejay, and his Uncle Skillet, the family's honorary drunk, frantically wave him over.

Jeezus, what now?

He makes his way over to the disruption.

"Nephuw," his uncle slurs, pointing his callused finger toward Shabbazz. "Tell yo' deejay pal over here dat he don't wanna mess wit' me! *Buuurp!* Hell, I wear draws older dan his youn' ass!"

"What's wrong?"

"I tell you whas wong, nephuwww. Yo' Moooslim pal is wong! I asked him to plah my song over an hour 'go and he refooses to play it! He hatin' on my song, nephuw!"

"Yo, Jay, no disrespect…" Shabbazz says while focusing on his laptop. "but could you take him somewhere else, he's messing with my flow–"

"You ain' *got* no dam flo', *BOY!*"

Uncle Skillet stumbles backward as Shabbazz mixes in GQ's dance hit, *Disco Nights*, and the crowd sings along–

"THE FEELIN'S RIGHT AND THE MUSIC'S TIGHT, ON A DISCO NII-II-IIIIIIGHT!"

The middle of the living room becomes swarmed with fresh old-school dancers.

James grabs his slouching uncle and guides him to the kitchen.

"He had nooo righ' talkin' to meeeee like that, *nephuwwww!*"

"It'll be alright. Let's get you somewhere where you can cool off."

They stumble into the kitchen where Tucker is helping Grace prep the lasagna and collard greens.

"B-But how the hell I-I'ma coo' off in dis hot-ass kitchen—?"

Skillet drops in a chair and passes out with his mouth wide open and arms spread downward.

"Oh my God!" Tucker covers her mouth in shock. "Is he alright?"

"He's fine." Grace ties her apron straps behind her body. "Give him fifteen minutes and he'll be up again, dancing and harassing somebody. Have you heard anything from your coworker, James?"

He lifts his uncle to a more comfortable position in the seat. "Not yet. I called her apartment this afternoon because she called in sick today and I didn't get an answer. I hope she's okay."

Tucker almost chokes on her drink.

"Are you alright?" Grace asks.

"Girl, I had one of those days which calls for a couple of shots of this right here." She raises her cup to Grace and takes another hefty gulp of her drink.

"Well, you'd better slow down before you wind up sitting right next to my brother with your mouth open like his."

"Y'ALL READY FOR THE CHA-CHA SLIDE!" blares out from the speakers in the other room.

Tucker's husband, Elliott, wearing a pair of Isaac Hayes glasses and a toothy grin, peeks inside of the kitchen.

"Let's cha-cha, baby!"

Tucker stands. "Y'all excuse me while I get my dance on."

"We're right behind you."

Elliott grabs his wife's hand and pulls her into the room.

James and Grace grab the rest of the food and they enter the living room.

"...SLIIIIIIDE TO THE LEFT! NOW SLIIIIIDE TO THE RIGHT! HANDS ON YOUR KNEES! HANDS ON YOUR KNEES! HOW LOW CAN YOU GO? CAN YOU GO DOWN LOW?"

"HOOOOOO!" the party people yell out, as they clumsily dance themselves into a delightful frenzy.

James sits the lasagna down, maneuvers his way through the dancers and onto the front porch where the postal crew is gulping down beers in the relaxing winter evening.

"What's up with the Knicks?" James asks.

"They lost," Roy deadpans. "Again."

"We need Ewing, Oakley, and Starks back, I don't care how old they are," grumbles Lou, sitting on the railing.

James points at the front door. "Man, y'all better get back in there before the food is all gone."

"What we need to do is make a beer run, like right now. I think I got the last one."

"You sure? We should have more in the garage cooler. I'll go check."

"Yo, is Cadina coming through?" Roy asks.

James checks his watch. "I texted her earlier, but didn't get any response, so I dunno."

Neville grins. "You didn't waste any time getting them digits, ain't that right, Playboy?"

"How else is she going to know how to get here? I told you about reaching, bruh."

"Get the fuck outta here," Lou smirks. You know you want that ass, Jay!"

"See, that's where your mind's at–"

"YOURS, TOO!" the crew laughs.

Roy points out into the street. "Yo, who's that pulling up?"

The crew turns their attention to the Porsche parking in James' driveway. A dapper-looking Freeman slides out of the passenger's seat and struts around to the driver's side to let Velour out.

She yells out to James, "You don't mind if I park here, do you? I don't want anyone bumping into my ride by accident."

"Nah, you good."

"Thanks." She turns her conceited grin to the rest of the crew. "Hey, y'all."

"Hey."

"James, now this is *nice*." Velour walks through the gate, admiring the building's brick exterior. As she walks up the porch steps, she purposely pulls off her beige chinchilla fur coat to reveal her voluptuous physique in a form-fitting, cream-colored, velvet mock-neck mini-dress, with the matching Manolo Blahnik pumps and purse.

She nods in approval. "You deserve this, man."

"Appreciate it. The food is ready, drinks are in the fridge, and don't forget to say 'Hey' to my moms."

"I won't." She turns to Freeman, excited. "I'm so ready to get our dance on!"

James greets Freeman and the smell of liquor hits him immediately. "I see you already got the party started."

"Man, I'm feeling nice right about now." Freeman laughs while unbuttoning his brown wool coat, exposing a cream-colored outfit that matches Velour's. "I'll be back out in a minute."

"No rush. We ain't going nowhere."

"Yo, Velour!" Lou circles around the gleaming Porsche. "Is this *you*?"

"Yes, Louis, it's my baby."

"How much did it set you back?"

She smiles. "It didn't set me back anything."

She sticks her hand out for Freeman to grab and they walk inside the house.

"Damn!" Roy stretches back onto the chair. "Velour looking kinda spicy tonight!"

"You saw the way she took off her fur so we could check out her assets, right?" Neville sits his empty beer bottle on the floor. "She knew what the hell she was doing."

"Yo, Jay!" Lou still walks around the Porsche. "Do you keep up with the overtime Velour be doing?"

"That's none of my business," James replies.

"I'm just asking because this right here ain't your everyday, run-of-the-mill Porsche."

"Like your ass is an expert on luxury cars," Neville jests.

"Actually, I am, Papa." Lou walks up to the porch. "That right there is the late model Porsche Cayenne Turbo S, with the twin-turbo engine that kicks out five hundred and fifty horsepower, *easy*. And those models *start* at a hundred and forty thousand. Google that shit, son."

"Maybe she's renting it for this weekend," Roy shrugs. "Because if it *is* hers, I can't imagine the car notes, especially with full insurance."

"I can't imagine affording something like that working at the post office, period," Neville burps. "*And* living in New York, too?"

"And *maybe* she has a budget plan." James turns to Neville. "None of us know her finances like that."

"True dat."

James' cousin, Garfield, sticks his head out the door. "Yo! We need to make a beer run, quick! Uncle Skillet is running through them!" Garfield closes the door.

James digs into his back pocket to fish out his wallet. "This don't make no damn sense."

"Man, put that away, we got this," Roy says.

"Can't do that. Y'all helped move all of my stuff, remember?"

"It's all good." Neville pulls out his truck keys. "We'll be back."

Lou points at James. "Tell 'Bazz I wanna hear some Biggie when we get back, not all of them damn line-dance songs."

James laughs. "Yeah, okay."

Lou and Roy pile into Neville's Jeep Cherokee, and they peel off down the street.

James pulls out his cell phone, searches for Cadina's number, and then dials it. As he waits for her to answer, the sudden thought of oxtails has him licking his lips.

CADINA

Camille backs her Yukon into their parents' driveway and automatically opens the cargo door. The sisters grab a couple of boxes containing the cooking ware and make their way towards the rear entrance of the house.

"Are you going straight to the party after you leave here?" Camille asks.

"Yes, Ma'am. I brought my outfit over the other night so I wouldn't have to go back to my apartment."

"Alright now." Camille unlocks the back door. "Got your little outfit ready, and the oxtails. My little sister is getting herself a man at this party!"

"Girl, I'm going to get my boogie on and have a good time."

"That's how it all starts, with a little bumpin' and grindin' on the dancefloor. Next thing you know, you're bringing home puppies!"

"You ain't right!"

The sisters laugh their way inside of the kitchen.

Cadina is surprised to find their parents sitting at the table in their nightclothes. "What's up?" she asks, placing the box on the countertop.

Camille retrieves a Tupperware bowl from the cabinet. "We have some good news to share with y'all!"

Vernon and Lorraine remain funeral quiet.

Camille scoops oxtails from the pan and into the bowl. "Well, let me be the first to say your daughter right here was the *bomb-diggy* at the birthday bash! She left such an impression on those rich folks that she has already established a clientele for future events! Now, tell me, how you like Cadina *now*?!?"

Cadina grins at her sister while rinsing out a pot.

"Why are y'all looking like that?" Camille asks their parents.

Cadina turns around.

She immediately cuts off the water.

Drying her hands, she analyzes her parents' vibe.

Vernon slouches in his chair while nursing a drink. His eyes remain glued to the table.

Meanwhile, Lorraine burns a hole right through Cadina's skull with laser red glare.

Something is not right.

Cadina tentatively asks, "Is there something wrong?"

"When it comes to you, Cadina, yes, there always seems to be something *wrong*." Lorraine pushes herself from the table. "But you don't seem to give a damn about anyone it affects, now do you?"

The sisters turn to each other, baffled.

"Wh-What is going on-?"

"You're such a project, young lady, that I wonder why we even devote our time and energy into making you a responsible woman!" Lorraine slowly marches right up to Cadina's face. Everything we build for you, you wind up tearing it down because you're just too damn selfish! Is this how we raised you, Cadina? To lie to us, to lie to your own *mother*? You better answer me when I ask you a question-"

"*Why are you coming at me like that? What did I do?*" Cadina shrieks, backpedaling.

"Didn't I say I was going to handle this?" Vernon calmly asks.

"She's my headache as well as yours, and she's making it painfully clear that your way is not working at all!"

"Everything will change, starting tonight. I promise you."

"Can somebody *please* tell me what's going on?" Cadina begs.

"I said what I had to say, now you have to deal with your father." Lorraine throws her hands in the air. "You've got me so burnt out,

I can't even look at you right now." Lorraine storms toward the kitchen door, and then turns around to yell, "*CAMILLE?*"

"Huh?"

"Leave," Vernon orders.

"Holla if you need me, girl."

Camille grabs her bowl and scurries from the kitchen.

Cadina is now alone with a man who habitually starts off all disputes with a glass of scotch.

"What did I do *this* time?"

Vernon finally lifts his head up from the table.

Bloodshot eyes narrowed in on her.

"You're really going to stand there and act oblivious to your mindless decisions?"

"Maybe if you tell me what I did or did not do, I can defend my actions-"

"Your assistant manager called me today."

Her body goes completely numb.

"She called…*you*."

"Denise Tucker, I believe her name was." He pauses for a moment. "And she had some rather disturbing news to share with me regarding your response to her station's policies."

She rolls her eyes and sighs. "Look, Dad, I know what I did was wrong—"

"Do you, *really*?" He raises his voice as he stands. "See, that's part of your problem right there! You seem to think that you can waltz into any environment with your own little set of rules and think everybody's supposed to abide by them? Little girl, you are so delusional-"

"Look, I asked this lady for the day off, in advance, mind you, so I could do this party. I even told her how important it was for me to attend, and she still told me no. So, yes, I took it upon myself to make a crucial decision. But like Cammy said; I was a *huge* success at this event!" Cadina pulls out an envelope from her dress coat to show her father. "A four-thousand-dollar *success*! And I'm sorry that I lied to Mommy, but I guarantee you this will never happen again—"

"There won't be a next time, Cadina...she fired you!"

Her face goes blank.

"What?"

"You heard me! You've been released!"

She hesitantly chuckles. "She's not gonna fire me for calling in sick, that's crazy—"

"What part are you not getting? She knew you weren't sick, that's why she called you directly, and then you had the audacity to hang up on her? What do you think was going to happen to you?"

His line of questioning has her unable to gather her thoughts.

"I really hate to say this about my own daughter, but you are becoming one bad investment! No matter what we do, or how many jobs we line up for you, you ruin every opportunity! You haven't been at the post office two weeks! Now, look what's happened!"

Her ringing cell phone halts Vernon's fury.

She fumbles in her coat pocket and answers the incoming call. "H-Hello?"

"How you doing, Cadina? It's James."

"Oh, hey."

"Saw your name on the call-in sheet this morning and felt the need to reach out to see how you were doing—"

"TELL WHOEVER THAT IS, THAT THIS IS A BAD TIME FOR YOU TO TALK, CADINA!" Vernon yells out at the top of his lungs.

Darting her eyes to her father, she whispers, "James, I have to call you back, okay?"

"Is everything alright?"

"HANG UP, NOW!"

"I'll call you back." She ends the call. "Was that really necessary?"

"What is necessary, Cadina, is for you to tell me how you're going to support yourself, moving forward." Vernon tightens the belt on his bathrobe. "Do you have a business plan laid out? Any future investors ready to back your so-called catering services? You must have something lined up for you to keep pulling stupid stunts like this! And you'd better figure out something real quick because the bills don't stop for anybody. Like your car I had to cosign for, your apartment I also had to cosign for. I cosigned my life away for you and this is how you repay me? So, I'll ask again; what are your *plans*?"

He doesn't wait for a response.

He walks over to the kitchen counter to pour himself another drink.

This bit of news cripple her all the way down on a nearby stool.

Her eyes begin to swell.

Just when she thought she was making great strides in redeeming her father's faith in her, she gives him another reason to distance himself even further because of her hollow promises. Her cavalier ways have finally run their course and she does not have a clue on how to reverse this agonizing misfortune.

He returns to the table with scotch and interrogation on the breath. "So, did you come up with a way to pay your bills legally or what?"

She snaps back into reality. "D-Did she really fire me?"

"I don't have time for games, Cadina; You have four grand to play with, but do you have an idea to build on?"

She lowers her head. "No."

"She fired you, alright, but I had to convince her to reconsider."

Her head springs up. "What?"

"To be more precise, after five minutes of listening to me *beg*, she found it in her heart to give you another chance. But this time around, you will have no room for error or bullshit. You have a lot of ground to cover as far as regaining your manager's trust, and the same goes for me, as well. Understood?"

Cadina wipes her eyes and nods her head in agreement.

"I can't hear you-"

"Yes, Sir."

He stands to his feet and then points down on the table. "Now is the time for you to start behaving like an adult or you will find yourself without a job or *me* to fall back on. It's time to grow the hell up, Cadina."

He downs the rest of his drink, slams the glass on the table, and staggers out of the kitchen.

Gravity has her pinned solidly to her stool.

At a sloth-like pace, she musters up enough strength to rise to her feet, gather her belongings, including the oxtails, and head out quietly through the back door and onto the driveway where she finds Camille sitting idly in her running truck.

Cadina slides the pan of oxtails in the backseat. She then squirms around to the passenger side of the Yukon. She sits there, staring through the windshield.

Staring through newly formed tears.

Camille rubs her sister's arm. "It's going to be okay."

"Could you do me a huge favor? Drop off the oxtails at James' place for me, please? I know it's out your way, but I'll pay for the gas expense-"

"Don't worry about that, girl, I got you." Camille backs out of the driveway and roars down the street. "But are sure you don't want to go? The atmosphere might do you a world of good."

"I can't. I-I totally forgot that my manager might be there and the last thing I need is to bump heads with her, you know what I mean?"

"Mmm-hmm," Camille double-takes her sister while driving. "Caddy..."

"I know, I know," Cadina chokes up. *"I just need to go home. Why do I keep fuckin' up like this, Cammy? I...I just can't-"*

The rest of her words never come.

She plants her face in her hands and her tear ducts release waves of guilt that have been nestled inside of her conscience for as long as she remembers.

Camille grabs her hand in comfort for the duration of the drive.

JAMES

*J*ames stares at his phone.
Who in the world was screaming in the background like that? He texts Cadina telling her to give him a call and then heads back into the house. He makes his way into the kitchen, checks on his wasted uncle who is now snoring, grabs a new garbage bag and returns to the living room to collect the trash. He trades a couple of jokes with his cousin Sabrina's attractive girl crew.

They laugh.

And flirt.

On any other occasion, he would have hollered at one of his cousin's friends without hesitation. Cadina, unknowingly, put an end to that.

Shabbazz gets the crowd buzzing again by mixing in the song, *Love Thang*, by First Choice, which causes James to turn around and shout out, "YEAH, BABY!" in approval. He dances over to the area where Divine and Elliott rule the spades table.

"BAM!" Divine shouts, slamming her big joker card down to win the last book of the game. As the losing team shake their heads and trot to the dance floor, another couple quickly fills their seats for a new game. James laughs as he drops their plates into the bag.

"You got next, James?" Divine begins shuffling the cards. "Or you don't want to be embarrassed in your new home? Which is it?"

"He doesn't want any of this, Dee." Elliott smiles while bouncing to the music.

"I got next, then," James says. "And I don't care who my partner is!"

"That's what I like! A man with confidence!"
Elliott fist bumps James.
"I'll be back. I'ma check on 'Nae."
"I forgot she was upstairs." Divine spreads her cards out in her hand. "Why isn't she down here partying with us?"
"Good question. I'll ask her."
James walks into the hallway and places the bag near the banister. He then trots up the staircase and knocks on Janae's bedroom door.
"Come in!" she yells.
Crossing the threshold, he pauses to soak in his daughter's customized new room. Posters of Beyonce and Destiny's Child hang on walls that are dominated by New York Knicks colors–blue, orange, and white. Basketball trophies, big and small, stand out everywhere. A smiling teddy bear the size of his daughter sits on a huge bean bag tucked away in the corner. On her computer desk are more championship medallions hanging from her LED-lighted vanity mirror. Lava lamps, a laptop, and a beautiful picture of Janae's mother, LaToya, in a standing glass frame, also accompany the sports medals.
James mentally pats himself on the back, pleased with the results.
But when he turns his head, his heart sinks.
Lying on her bed, dressed in a purple Nike jumpsuit with both legs and arms crossed, Janae watches a music video on the wall-mounted flat screen. In the video, a rapper is squatting on top of a Mercedes Maybach with a cigar in one hand while flashing money with the other. Right beside the car is her mother, LaToya, dressed in a skimpy outfit and positioning herself in sexy poses.
His daughter must have watched this same video a hundred times.
And each time, it produces the same outcome.
More inquiries about a person Janae hardly knows.
"What other videos has Mommy been in?" she asks.

Here we go.

James walks over and cops a squat at the end of the bed. His eyes scroll her face.

No signs of happiness anywhere in her inquiry. Only curiosity.

"Now, that's a good question. I know of only three off the top of my head. You want to call her and ask-"

"I tried…went straight to voicemail."

Her response was as cold as it was distant.

Just like her mother's presence in her life.

Then, out of the blue, a smile appears on her face. Her eyes land on him. "Mommy said one day she will be the star of her own videos."

For the past two years, something as simple as a smile has been a rare commodity for his daughter to express. And she possesses such a beautiful one. He hopes it stays for a while.

"Yep. That's always been her priority." He puts on a happy face and asks, "You wanna swing by her place tomorrow after church? I'll drop you off and pick you up later in the evening?"

"Why bother? She'll only drop me off at Aunt Tasha's afterward like she did the last three times."

Her empty expression returns twofold.

She points the remote toward the flat screen and switches to a basketball game.

James remains upbeat. "Why don't you come down to the party and show everybody how to do the real Stanky Leg dance. And we could do it together, like this…"

James shoots up from the bed and clumsily performs the dance routine. She finally belts out a sincere laugh.

"Dad, that dance is so old. And you're doing it wrong."

"Whatever. Come downstairs with me."

"I don't feel like being sociable tonight, I'm sorry."

"No, no, that's fine."

"But can I eat up here while I watch tv? I promise I won't mess up my new room."

"I'll bring you up a plate and a food tray."
"Thanks, Daddy."
The doorbell rings.
About time, Cadina.
"Love you."
"Love you more."
Janae smiles while turning to the game.

James leaves the room and whistles down the staircase. The music pounding from the living room increases his nervousness. He checks himself in the mirror while trying to tame the butterflies circling around in his stomach.

Calm your ass down, Soldier, Cadina's just another woman.
But she is so pretty, though.
And cool as hell.
He takes a deep breath, opens the door...
...and receives one helluva surprise.

Standing in front of him, in a slimmer version of her former self, is Lovelle, who sports a thick, tan poncho that works perfectly with her black Chico jeans and black knee-high Milano boots. In front of her, she holds a gift bag with both hands.

"Hey, James!" she says, brimming with excitement.

He does a couple of fast double-takes inside the crowded living room to see if Freeman and Velour are visible. Lovelle steps inside the foyer and gives him a hug.

"What a surprise!" he says, meaning every word. "How are you?"

"I'm doing well, and it's good to see you! It's been a minute."

"I know." James maintains an exaggerated smile as his eyes ping-pong from Lovelle to the living room, then back to Lovelle. "I must say you're looking very nice tonight."

"Why, thank you!"

"I see you still hitting the gym. Arms all toned and everything..."

"Man, you made my day!" Her full bob hairdo bounces as she laughs. "I can't go back to old habits, my spirit won't allow it, so yes, hitting the gym every day is my new therapy and I feel great. Very proud of myself."

"That's good, that's good." James continues to stall, unsure what to do.

She extends the gift bag towards him. "I got you a little something for the house."

"Awww, thanks, but you didn't have to."

"Now, you know I wasn't coming over here empty-handed."

Suddenly, it dawned on him.

How did she know about the housewarming? Because I know damn well Freeman didn't invite her over here-

Divine rushes into the foyer with arms spread wide to hug Lovelle.

"Hey, girl!" she screams over the music. "I thought you'd never get here!"

James cuts his eyes at the instigator–Divine.

She returns a *yeah-I-invited-her* smile right back at him.

"You know I wasn't going to miss out on this!" Lovelle begins to wiggle her body to Sean Paul's song, *Like Glue*. "It sure is live up in here!"

"Well, let's get it in!"

Lovelle begins to two-step into the noisy living room. She cheeses at James. "I can't wait to see the rest of the house, James!"

No you don't, Lovelle.

"You're going to love it, trust me!" assures Divine.

They enter the packed living room.

Lovelle stops dead in her tracks.

"What's wrong?" Divine asks.

Don't act stupid, Dee.

James knows exactly what is wrong and so does she.

He follows Lovelle's gaze through the dancing couples, to the speaker by the wall. They all witness Freeman and Velour erotically slow-grinding against the wall as if it was a horizontal bed. But the ultimate stab is when Freeman deep-throats Velour with his tongue and she sucks on it as if it was an icicle pop.

From the corner of his eye, James sees Lovelle's bottom lip quivering from hurt.

She spins around, grabs Divine by the arm, and drags her back into the foyer.

He reluctantly follows them.

"Is this your idea of a sick joke, Dee?" Lovelle growls as she maintains a firm hold onto Divine's arm. "You told me your brother was looking forward to seeing *me* tonight! Who the hell is *she*?"

"Her name is Velour. She's our coworker."

"*Coworker*? She *works* with y'all?" Lovelle spins around. "Y'all knew about her all this time and then gonna smile in my face like everything is cool? *James*?"

His mouth opens but nothing comes out.

Instead, Divine does all the talking.

"Look, Lovelle, I'm sorry I lied to you, but I'm sick and tired of him playing you for a fool! Y'all are supposed to be getting married in six months. Does that look like someone who's ready to tie the knot in six months–"

"First of all, Dee, I do not appreciate you inviting me over here to be embarrassed–"

"That was never my intention, and you know this! I'm trying to help you see the light–"

"I am very capable of handling my own affairs, okay?" Lovelle lowers her tone. "You're my girl and all, Dee, but at this moment, you're about as full of shit as your brother in there."

"Come on now–"

"Enjoy your party, *James*."

Lovelle storms out the front door.

Right on her heels is Divine, vehemently trying to further explain her bold decision.

He walks out on the porch to get some air.

Instinctively, he pulls out his phone and dials Cadina's number.

It goes straight to voicemail.

Maybe she is not coming after all.

James pockets his phone while witnessing Lovelle slamming her car door in Divine's face and peeling off into the night.

Divine marches up the steps with an attitude.

"That wasn't cool what you did, Dee. And you made me look like a fool on top of it."

"Why is Freeman throwing away his relationship with Lovelle, just for a jump-off?" Divine stuffs her hands inside the pouch of her sweatshirt. "Because that's all Velour really is. I don't understand how it even got to this point."

"Maybe it's not for you to understand. What you need to do is fall back and let them handle their problems... and not become one. Ever thought of that?"

"Well, when the both of them stop coming to me like I'm their mediator, then I might just do that."

She walks past James and heads back into the house.

James inhales the cold air and blows out heated frustration. What was supposed to be an evening filled with joy and happiness has now taken a sour detour and the one person who he was hoping would swing through to brighten his mood won't even bother to return his phone call.

The postal crew return from the beer run, with each person carrying two twenty-four packs through the gate.

"You can never have enough, baby!" Neville walks inside the house.

"Any lasagna left? A brother is *starving!*" Roy asks.

"I don't know, man," James responds, "Look on the table in there."

James and the rest of the crew make their way inside and is loudly welcomed in by the classic oldie, *You're Gonna Miss My Lovin'.*

Lou almost drops his beer. "Oh, HELLS no! I wanna hear some Biggie, like right now!"

The fed-up Latino sits his case of beer down to have a word with his deejay friend.

Meanwhile, Uncle Skillet blasts from out of the kitchen, singing along with Lou Rawls, *"WHEN IT'S COLD OUTSIIIIIDE! TURN THAT SHIT UP, MOOOSLIM!",* at the top of his lungs while grabbing Tucker's hand to dance.

Grace walks up to James with a food plate. "This is for 'Nae. Try to get her to come downstairs and see her family."

"I tried earlier." James takes the plate and grabs a food tray from the rack. "But she's in her missing-her-mommy mood."

"I hate that this woman has scarred her like that." Grace shakes her head. "But we're going to have our day in court, mark my word."

"The countdown has already begun."

Grace nods. She returns to the living room and starts to dance along with Tucker and Skillet.

James heads up the staircase, wondering if he should make one last call to Cadina–

Crash!

What the hell...

James quickly sits the plate and tray down on the top of the staircase and rushes into Janae's room.

His eyes zig-zag around the area until they land on his daughter.

Tears race down her face as she stares downward.

His eyes continue traveling towards the hardwood floor.

He now sees the source of the noise.

LaToya's picture, which was neatly framed in a standing holder, now lay underneath shards of glass that can puncture deeply if Janae was to make one wrong step.

"I don't want her staring at me anymore!"

She begins trembling and breathing uncontrollably.

Her voice crackles when she attempts to speak again.

"I-I...don't...want..h-her...looking...at..."

James tiptoes around the shattered glass and scoops up Janae who continues to sob on his shoulders.

He collapses down on the bed.

They both hold onto each other tightly.

"Why doesn't she like me, Daddy?" Janae squeals. "I didn't do anything to her! I didn't do NOTHING to her!"

"Now, don't say that." He tightens his hug on her. "You know your mother loves you-"

"She doesn't act like it! She never acts like it! How am I supposed to love her back? How, Daddy?"

This hurts him to the core.

He lets her vent. She needs this time to purge.

It has been long overdue.

He rocks her back and forth and stares at the shattered image of LaToya laying on the floor while Lou Rawls' timeless oath seeps into his daughter's sanctuary.

"I know, I know, I know, that you are gonna miss my lovin'..."

FREEMAN

Stephanie Mills' quiet storm classic, *Secret Lady*, along with burning lemon lavender Yankee Candles, enhance the cozy atmosphere swirling around Freeman's living room.

Velour pours pineapple Ciroc in both glasses. They toast the evening, take sips, and she lays her head on Freeman's lap.

She suddenly cracks up. "Now, what was up with James' uncle? What's his name, Skeeter or something?"

"Skillet..." Freeman laughs. "They call him Skillet."

"Yo, when he spilled beer on Shabbazz's equipment, I just knew it was about to go down!"

"Skillet's mission was sabotage. He wanted Lou Rawls in heavy rotation."

"Yes, he did!" She winces while rubbing her feet. "I don't know how I left home without my flats, knowing I was going to be dancing. Now, my feet are paying for it."

"Corns screaming, huh?"

"Please. I do not possess any corns on my feet, okay?"

"I'll be the judge of that. Swing them bad boys over here."

She turns her body around and places her feet on his lap. He grabs the Jergens lotion from the nearby corner table, applies a small amount in his hands, and rubs them vigorously before going to work on her feet.

His massaging conjures soft moans from the diva.

She leans her head straight back.

Perky nipples indent the top of her dress.

Blond hair dangles in elation.

His manhood awakens.

She props her head on her hand and smiles at him through inebriated eyes. "You know, if you ever get tired of working at the p.o., this could definitely be your primary gig."

He grins. "I see the Ciroc got you talking crazy."

"Honey, I am not that drunk. You do have amazing hands."

"Then I will accept the compliment."

"As you should."

She takes another sip from the glass. She never lifts her eyes off him.

His manhood wants to stand at attention so badly.

At ease, Soldier.

"Can I ask you a personal question?"

"What's up?"

"Did you give up on church altogether because of your mother's passing?"

He reads her expression. She is sincere with her query.

Still, he shrugs while tending to her feet.

"I can understand if you don't want to talk about it—"

"No, no, it's cool." He realizes she is right. "I mean, other factors contributed as well, but that was a huge part of it, you know?"

She nods.

"My moms was one of God's true soldiers, for real. She helped our pastor build the church to the successful ministry it has become today. She sang in the choir, taught Sunday school, she was a deaconess, you name it, she did it and with pure intentions. It wasn't until recently that I had to face the fact that God relieved her from her duties here on earth." His words came out more somber than he intended. "You know, besides James, I really haven't had another person to share this whole crazy ordeal with."

"Wow. I feel honored." She rubs his hands. "I know it was hard."

"Time heals all wounds, right? I'ma be alright."

He stares at her, unsure about bringing up a particular topic, but decides to ask her, anyway.

"That night, when I dropped you off at your place after the show, things got a little heated with you and your brother as I was leaving."

She immediately grabs her drink.

She does not sip, this time. She gulps it all the way down.

Obviously, he had struck a nerve.

She smiles defensively. "I was wondering if you were going to bring that up."

"The way he was yelling at you, how could I not."

"It was just a brother and sister misunderstanding. No big deal."

"Let me guess. He wasn't exactly thrilled about you bringing company over to his humble abode."

Velour does not answer quickly.

Instead, she pours another round for them both.

She goes back to nursing her drink. "You can say that."

"I figured as much."

"Don't get me wrong, Vincent is very out-going and loves company. We just caught him at a bad time, but he was cool afterward."

"Any thoughts about getting your own place?"

Freeman caught it.

It was very subliminal, but she disguised it quickly with a drunken cackle.

Apparently, he touched another nerve when she flashed a dark look that lasted about a nano-second before the chuckling began.

Maybe he should not have brought it up.

But he is glad he did.

Velour brings the glass to her lips. "I don't see that happening any time soon."

"Oh, my bad. We're living in mansions and shit."

She almost spits out her drink in laughter. "*Noooo*, that's not the reason..."

He raises an eyebrow at her while massaging.

She sighs. "Well, it's not the *only* reason, okay? I love the quiet neighborhood we live in. We're not that far from Manhattan and we're like two minutes from City Island and you *know* how I love my seafood, so I like my situation. Is that a crime?"

"But it's not *your* place. No matter how big and fancy it may be, you have limitations placed on you if the owner is not in the mood...like, for example, inviting your friends over."

"I can always come here."

"Is that right?"

"Unless your fiancée has a say so in the matter."

He stops rubbing her feet.

"I like how you spun this whole conversation around, you ain't slick–"

She laughs. "I'm just saying! She may have reservations about my presence here."

"See, now, that's where you're wrong. *I'm* the master of this here domain."

"*Really?*"

"Yes, *really*. I pay the rent in this mofo."

She places her drink on the table and leans toward him.

"Well, the master has to make a decision tonight on what he really wants."

"Excuse me?"

She leans in closer.

Alcohol and sex on the tongue.

"My time is valuable, Freeman. And I play second fiddle to no one. So, what's up?"

She frees a foot from his hand and uses it to massage his manhood.

A huge bulge appears in his pants.

She means what she says.

"And what makes you think I haven't made my decision already?"

"I don't go by a person's word, Freeman. I need receipts."

"It's like that, huh..."

"Yep."

Freeman leisurely moves his hands up her legs.

She accommodates him by inching up her mini dress just enough for her cream thong to be exposed. His left-hand stays on course towards her love canal. Then, using two of his fingers, he slides the thong to the side while allowing the other fingers to enter her moistened tunnel.

"How is *this* for receipts?"

She grins wickedly. "Sliding your fingers inside my coochie hardly qualifies, Boo."

Yet, she widens her legs for easy access.

The gentle rubbing and probing with his fingers produce waterfalls of pure ecstasy.

Her head falls back onto the edge of the couch.

She closes her eyes and bites her bottom lip.

She moans and squirms in delight.

His manhood is now officially rock-hard.

"You did say my hands were amazing."

"*Oh, God*, I did say that, right?"

She lunges herself on top of him. He hurries to unbutton his dress shirt. She aggressively throws her tongue down his mouth as they begin rolling around on the living room rug. She spreads his shirt apart so she can suck on his hairy nipples. From there, her tongue slopes down to his belly button. Freeman fights with his belt buckle until it comes apart. As soon as he pulls his pants down, he hears the front door unlocking and opening, only to be stopped by the door chain.

"SHIT!"

He jumps to his feet, yanks his pants back up, and fastens his belt buckle.

Velour calmly pulls her dress back down. She then sits on the couch with her legs crossed, while retrieving her drink.

"Expecting company?" She giggles between sips.

BOOM! BOOM! BOOM! BOOM! BOOM!

"I KNOW YOU'RE IN THERE! OPEN THE DAMN DOOR!"
BOOM! BOOM! BOOM! BOOM! BOOM!

"Do you want me to leave?"

Freeman wipes his face with both hands. "No."

He takes a deep breath, and then clumsily advances to the front entrance.

He cracks the door open with the chain still attached.

The anger scorches from Lovelle's glare.

"Oh, so we're leaving chains on the door now, Freeman?"

"Look, this is not a good time—"

"When is it ever a good time, you tell me?" Her tone is more hurtful than angry. "I saw you at the party with your *coworker* and I really don't care if she's in there. WE need to talk, so open this damn door! Now!"

He has been avoiding this moment for months.

The moment of transparency.

He closes the door, slides off the chain, and then re-opens it.

Lovelle barges inside of the small entrance. She then makes her way into the living room and embarrassingly soaks in all the venereal stimulation that has been left lingering in the air.

Velour places her glass down on the table and stands.

Lovelle eyeballs her from head to toe.

The quiet tension hangs like a London fog.

Freeman clears his throat. "Uh, Lovelle, Velour. Velour, Lovelle-"

"What *part* of me even suggests that I wanted to know her fuckin' name, Freeman?" Lovelle tightens up on her purse handle. "I came here to talk to *you*! Not to get to know *her*! Let's be clear!"

Freeman and Velour trade glances.

Velour then picks up a Vibe magazine from the table. "I'ma, uh, go in the other room and let you two talk."

Velour shuffles barefoot to the back room.

Freeman swings around to Lovelle.

"First of all, coming in here all swoll and yelling at everybody is gonna get your ass out that door that much quicker, a'ight? So, bring it all the way down-"

"Was it *her* you took to the show, Freeman?" She points towards the back room. "With the tickets *I* bought you?"

"Yes! And if I remember correctly, you gave me the tickets to do whatever *I* wanted to do with them—"

"I bought those tickets for *us*, fool! Not for you to escort some high-yellow heffa! You think I'm that simple?"

"You never made it clear to me, so whose fault is that?"

"This is pathetic, man!"

She plops down on his couch and buries her face in her hands. Tears leak between her fingers.

His breathing calms down. He takes a seat next to her.

"How long have you two been involved?" she asks, speaking through her hands.

He had to think about it for a second. "Just happened recently."

The silence is dense between the two.

She brings her wet face around to his. "So, is this temporary, permanent, which is it?"

He takes a deep breath. "I don't know."

"Are you breaking up with me, Freeman?"

Her eyes are filled with dreaded anticipation.

"You really want me to answer that?"

"The *answer* just jiggled her behind into your bedroom!" she points. "But I'm giving you the opportunity to be a man and tell me where the hell this relationship is going!"

He stands and points his finger directly in her face.

"Oh, just like I should've given you the opportunity to tell me where you were the day my mother got killed, right? We're talking about that kind of opportunity?"

The power of speech is snatched from her throat.

She turns away from him.

He could not keep it bottled in any longer.

Now it was his time to vent.

She faces him. Voice shaking in guilt. "So, this is your way of getting back at me for what I did? We went over this a thousand times-"

"And I'm *still* bringing the shit up!" he roars. "You shed some pounds and then you lose your fuckin' mind, in the process? I'm calling you about my mom's passing and where were you? Huh? WHERE WERE YOU? And you had the nerve to let that nigga answer your *phone*? How am I supposed to forget that shit? And then you try to put the blame on me for not spending enough time with you, yet I'm busting my ass at work doing overtime just to buy that damn ring? I bet you didn't tell the Pastor that part, did you? Trying to be faithful to you and then you decide to get brand new on *me*? You played your own self, big time!"

She tries her best to contain her emotions.

He does a good job controlling his.

"Do you want another apology from me, Freeman? Fine. I'm *sorry*. I'm so sorry for messing up everything between us! I'm owning up to my mistake because I love you so much and want us to continue moving forward with our lives-"

"Oh, we're gonna move forward alright, but it won't be together."

"Why you *say* that?"

"Because after my moms' funeral, we still carried on as if nothing ever happened and that wasn't fair for either of us." He sits down next to her. "Now, I owe it to myself to figure out what I really want in my life. And that requires some space from you. I'm sorry."

An avalanche of tears rolls down her cheeks.

She grabs his hand. "I don't wanna lose you-"

"You're saying that out of guilt, Lovelle." He pulls his hand away. "You need this time yourself to figure out if you're really ready to settle down with someone. And I just don't see that happening."

"But I'm *telling* you right now-"

"Lovelle...let's not be redundant. I said my piece. Now, do us both a favor and go home."

"Go *home*? As much money as I've invested decorating this apartment, this *is* my home! *She* needs to go!"

"I'm not going back and forth with you, Lovelle. Leave…right now!"

They glare at each other for a hot five seconds.

In a low spiteful voice, Lovelle says, "Okay…that's how you wanna do this? Fine."

She pulls off the ring. She shoves it, along with the apartment key, into his hand.

She stands, grabs her purse, and points at him. "Have fun with your little coworker, if that's what you really want, I *know* the shit is temporary…because what we've built together over the years, Freeman, you just don't throw away over a piece of ass."

"But that's exactly what you did when you took 'ole boy to the hotel. Now, get the fuck out of my apartment!"

She stares him down before wiping her face and stomping down the hallway. She slams the door with enough authority to wake up the entire Co-op City area.

Freeman drops back down on the sofa.

He grabs the Ciroc bottle from the table and sucks it dry.

For months, he has tried to mask his hurt by either drinking his sorrows away or by absorbing all the overtime he could muster from his job. But the gut-wrenching pain of his fiancée admitting she was having an affair with another guy still reeked in his memory bank like fresh dog shit on a hot summer day. And with his mother passing around the same time, the emotional effort he put into working things out with Lovelle was about as mechanical as an assembly line. His clouded mind no longer needs the aggravation from her. What he needs now is instant healing from those painful memories.

The sound of Velour's footsteps breaks his chain of thoughts.

With her heels on, purse in hand, and fur underneath her arm, she smiles sympathetically while gently combing through his afro with her soft fingers.

The instant healing process begins.

"You alright?" she softly asks.

"Had better moments. Where are you off to?"

"Anywhere but here," she chuckles. "No offense, Freeman, but she might come back with a shotgun to take care of some unfinished business. *And* reclaim that ring. May I see it?"

He hands it to her.

She holds it up in the air. "I see you know your diamonds...I'm impressed."

"I stayed within my budget."

She gives the ring back to him. "It's beautiful."

"Thanks." He twirls the ring between his fingers before placing it next to the lamp. "But I seriously doubt she's coming back here." He grabs and holds her hand. "Stay. Please."

She mulls for a moment. "Okay. But if she comes back acting crazy, I will jump out that window, Bionic Woman-style."

His laughter triggers a sharp pain that shoots through his already swirling head. He rubs his head and eyes.

"What's wrong?"

"Ohhhh, nothing. Just my head trying to explode, that's all. Too much drama, too much of that pineapple shit..." he laughs, causing another sharp attack.

She throws her fur and purse on the couch and rubs his forehead. "Do you have any aspirin?"

"Motrins in the bathroom cabinet."

"Two Motrins coming right up." She hurries to the bathroom.

The migraine subsides, mercifully. He walks over to gaze out the window. Looking through the blinds, he notices Lovelle's Honda Accord still parked outside. He glances around the area, wondering where she is.

"Do you think this will cure that headache?"

Freeman turns around. "Well, I hope it does—"

Those were the only words that left his mouth.

Posing near the entertainment system is Velour, now dressed in a cream-colored, two-piece velvet lingerie set that shows off her butter-toned, hourglass figure.

"Are you ready to take your medicine now?"

Her velvet thong flosses between her golden round buttocks as she saunters towards him. She grabs a hold of his hand and guides him back to the sofa. She makes him sit down and then places two Motrin pills in his palm.

His manhood is ready to pop out of his pants.

"You know I'm going to need something to wash these down with."

She smiles ever so lovely while pushing her breasts in his face. "Not when you have *these* to suck on to create your own juices."

"You're just full of surprises tonight, aren't you?"

Velour straddles his lap. She places her finger on his mouth, telling him to, "*Shhhh.*"

She pops out one bouncy breast. She takes one of the pills from his hand and balances it on her bite-sized nipple.

She whispers, "Now open wide."

Freeman hungrily attacks the medicated tit and sucks it like a newborn child.

"*Ooooooh, yessssss...*"

She pulls out the other breast and repeats the performance. He continues tongue-kissing both throbbing nipples until her tongue meets him halfway and together, they embrace one another with unbridled passion and desire. He grabs both of her butt cheeks and begins to dry-hump Velour, who in return, cradles his head for ample support. The power of his hammer desperately tries to bust out of his zipper each time she breathes and moans in his face. As both sets of hands begin to rip off his pants, he suddenly stops.

"What's wrong, Baby?" she asks, sucking feverishly on his neck.

"My blinds."

Velour turns around and notices the window blinds are wide open. She turns back around and says, "What about 'em?"

Freeman laughs. "So, you don't mind if somebody from the building across the street decides to videotape us?"

Kissing his lips, she coos, "Wouldn't that be exciting..."

"I see you're the adventurous type." He sucks on her lips. "But tonight, I just want it to be me and you, not the whole boogie-down Bronx, a'ight?"

She laughs. "Fine with me. I'll get the blinds; *you* just take those pants off."

Her cat-like stroll toward the window has him snatching off the rest of his clothes and flinging them every which way in the living room. He then leans butt-naked on the couch and wrestles with the condom package. He notices her peering out the window for a mighty long time.

"Something caught your eye out there, or you just like the idea of having the moon shine on your ass?"

She folds the blinds and then flicks the lights off.

Traces of the moon's afterglow spotlights half of her glossy-toned body as she catwalks back over to him. She then slips out of her thong and bra set, fully exposing the delicious set of twins that stand firm and round on their very own. She kneels in front of his stiff soldier, snatches the condom package from his hand, and says, "I was thinking about how happy I am in your company right now."

He reads the genuineness deep within her eyes.

Feels it with her delicate touches.

She rips the condom bag open with her teeth and then pulls out its contents.

"*Very* happy," she softly repeats, with Gladys Knight's, *If I Were Your Woman*, chiming in the background.

As she deep-throats her way into a world of happiness, Freeman lay back, closes his eyes, and tells himself how happy *he* is that the two headaches he was suffering from, (the one beating inside his head and the other named Lovelle), are nullified by Velour's very presence.

This is the moment they have been craving for the past two months.

They sex each other to the break of dawn.

LOVELLE TAYLOR

"*A*re you alright, young lady?"

Lovelle sits at the bottom of the building's staircase, head hanging, shoulders slumped, lost in a world filled with despair. She turns around to the voice of an old man carrying a garbage bag, staring down at her. Apparently, she is blocking traffic. She pushes herself from the steps.

"I'm fine, Sir."

"You don't look it."

The old man bristles before heading out the front entrance.

She pulls out her compact mirror. *Damn*. She stares at raccoon-looking eyes that washed away make-up and eyeliner hours ago with the last of her tears.

The old man was right. She looks like a hot mess.

She sighs before grabbing her purse and heading out the front door.

She manages to walk to her car with her head held high, only to conceal a heart that has become a wounded beneficiary ever since she stormed out of Freeman's apartment. She can still feel the harsh effects of his flaming anger. And she has nobody to blame but herself.

She wanted so badly to receive validation from him about her recent weight loss, but she never received it the way she envisioned. He was always tired from working many hours at the post office. So, her ego found someone else to fill that void. A dude at the gym, who was all too willing to show her how much he admires a woman "who takes care of herself."

The affair lasted only two sessions.

But it was the last session when she would receive that fateful phone call.

She was devastated by the horrific news about Freeman's mother.

But also embarrassed by getting caught.

And she was supposed to be a saved woman.

Truth be told, Freeman had always loved her, despite the weight. *She* was the one with the insecurity issues, so she expected him to over-compensate for her lack of self-love. Now stuck with the reality of losing the man once deemed by her parents "a godsend", she has no other choice but to leave her burdens with God because she got caught up in her own low-carb hype.

Opening the car door, her instincts prompt her to look up at the second-floor window to Freeman's apartment.

And when she does, she receives the mother of all surprises.

Sneering through the cracked blinds is Velour, watching *her* with hawk-like precision, all the while, exposing her bare essence.

Lovelle stands paralyzed, with her mouth wide open.

Velour squeezes her breasts and blows a kiss directly her way.

No, that bitch didn't!

And just like that, the blinds close shut, and the lights go off in the background.

Lovelle must have blinked twenty times in humiliation.

"Are you sure you're okay, young lady?"

She spins around.

The old man again.

This time, she shoots a hostile glare at him before collapsing into her Honda. Mashing the gas pedal, she makes a promise to herself to never step foot on this block for as long as she lives.

AND NOW A SNEAK PEEK FROM POSTAL II REDEMPTION AVAILABLE NOW...

FREEMAN

*F*reeman downs his water as another postal truck pulls up and parks in the spot where Cadina's truck had been. Bouncing out of the passenger's side is a person he has not seen since the early part of the year.

Freeman shouts, "You know you can't park there, that's for working people!"

Dante welcomes him with a bear hug. "What's good, baby?" He slaps Freeman's back as hard as he can.

"Chillin', chillin'. I haven't seen you in a minute! How's parcel post treating you?"

"Man, everything's gravy." Dante uses a damp rag to wipe over a bald head that used to sport a short fade. "Those Amazon packages got a brother humping all around Manhattan, you know what I'm saying? But I'm lovin' it, though. How's everything going between you and Velour?"

Freeman can't help but smile. "Man, she's been spoiling a brother *rotten*. I mean, she practically insists on handling all the tedious work, like the return to sender mail, the forwardable mail, she breaks down the parcels, plus all the mail sweeps…I'm surprised you wanted to leave that kind of support."

"I know, but it was time to move on, that's how the universe works. I got what I wanted, you got what you needed, and she got *you*, in more ways than one."

"Don't start that mess. I hear enough of that upstairs."

"I bet you do!" Dante playfully taps Freeman's chest. "But yo, let me handle my business so I can get out of this heat! It's hotter than *twelve* muthafuckas out here."

"Who you telling? I'm out. Peace!"

Dante opens the back of his truck.

Freeman throws his backpack over his shoulder, takes a couple of steps, and then turns back around. "Yo, Dante…"

Dante closes his cargo door, and then pushes his tub of parcels over to him. "What's up?"

"You remember Ms. Phillips; she lives in the 200 building?"

"Apartment 6D, yeah. Why, what's up?"

"Has she ever complained to you about someone using her credit cards?"

"Nah, man, can't say that she has." Dante ponders for a moment. "Someone messing with her mail like that?"

"She said it happened three times in the past two months. Velour says she's not playing with a full deck and to just ignore her."

"Well, if that's what Velour said, then you don't have anything to worry about, right?"

"I guess not. Yo, be good."

Freeman heads down the block, wondering whether he should grab a hotdog from the street vendor.

"Yo, Free!"

He turns around.

His heart skips a major beat.

Just a minute ago, Dante's whole demeanor was bigger than life itself.

The expression he bears now is the polar opposite.

Absolute fear.

"What's up?" *What's wrong with you?* is the question Freeman really wanted to ask.

For what seemed like an eternity, Dante finally answers. "Ah, nothing. Just be careful."

Freeman squints from the sun. "Careful about what?"

Another long, drawn-out pause controls Dante's speech. "Home. Just be careful going home, that's all. I'll holla at you later."

And just like that, the toothy grin reappears on Dante's face as he pushes the tub of parcels into Midway station.

Freeman stands idle, trying to digest what just happened.

Just be careful.

Did he really mean to be careful going home?

Or something else?

Freeman lets it go. When he bumps into Dante again, maybe he will inquire more about it. He stops at the vendor to purchase two icy bottled waters instead of the hotdog he was craving. He guzzles one of the bottles with the quickness and takes his sticky body down the subway stairs.

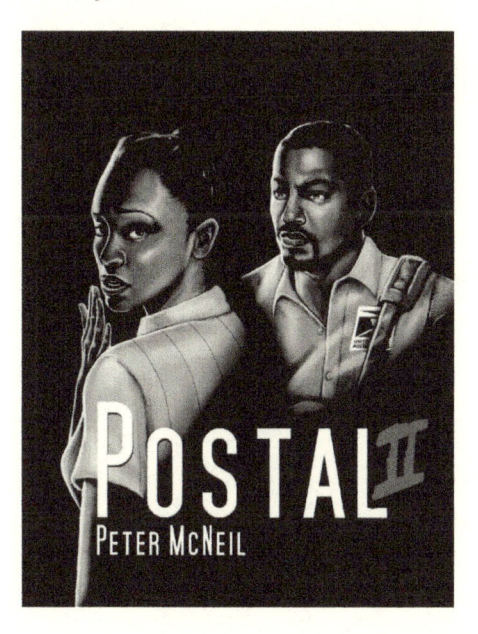

POSTAL II

PETER MCNEIL

ABOUT THE AUTHOR

PETER McNEIL, novelist and filmmaker was born in Brooklyn, New York and now resides in Charlotte, North Carolina with his wife Pamela and three young adults, Justin, Jordan, and Milahn. His inspiration to narrate compelling stories derived from the socially conscious filmmaker Spike Lee and the legend of horror novels, Stephen King. He formed A Brighter Path Productions to self-publish his novels and finance his film projects. Navigating in the film and literary arena, he felt it was important to take ownership of his content while also conveying universal messages that will have a global impact.

"I take my craft seriously so I can give you the best work possible. I appreciate you taking the time out of your busy schedule to read anything I've created, so honest feedback will allow me to continue to grow as a writer. Stay blessed."

Pete McNeil

Made in the USA
Middletown, DE
26 September 2025